The Atherton Pack, Book 1

Toni Griffin

About the eBook You Have Purchased:

This copy is intended for the original purchaser of this ebook ONLY. No part of this ebook may be reproduced, scanned, or distributed in any printed or electronic form without prior written permission from the authors. Please do not participate in or encourage piracy of copyrighted materials in violation of the author's rights. Purchase only authorized editions.

Cover Artist: Freddy MacKay
Editor: Erika Orrick

Second Edition

LIAM: THE ATHERTON PACK, BOOK 1 © 2014 Toni Griffin
All Rights Reserved.
Published in the United States of America.

ALL RIGHTS RESERVED: *Liam: The Atherton Pack, Book 1* is a work of fiction. Names, places, characters, and incidents are either the product of the author's imagination or are fictionalized. Any resemblance to any actual persons, living or dead, is entirely coincidental. The story contains explicit sexual content and is intended for adult readers.

Any person depicted in the Licensed Art Material is a model and is being used solely for illustrative purposes.

PUBLISHER
Mischief Corner Books, LLC

Dedication

For everyone who kept asking me for more wolves, I hope you enjoy Liam's story.

Trademarks Acknowledgement

The author acknowledges the trademarked status and trademark owners of the following wordmarks mentioned in this work of fiction:

DeLonghi Nespresso: DeLonghi Appliances SRL
Viagra: Pfizer Inc.
Kmart (Australia): Wesfarmers
iPod: Apple Inc.
CWA: Country Women's Association of Australia

Table of Contents

[Title](#)
[Copyright](#)
[Dedication](#)
[Trademarks Acknowledgement](#)
[Chapter One](#)
[Chapter Two](#)
[Chapter Three](#)
[Chapter Four](#)
[Chapter Five](#)
[Chapter Six](#)
[Chapter Seven](#)
[Chapter Eight](#)
[Chapter Nine](#)
[Chapter Ten](#)
[Epilogue](#)
[Dear Reader](#)
[About Toni Griffin](#)
[Also by Toni Griffin](#)
[About Mischief Corner Books](#)

Chapter One

Another week passed with Saturday night arriving as it invariably did, and Declan Morgan once again found himself alone. Sometimes the fact he had no friends really bothered him. He had a younger brother, Tommy, and they were close, but the ten-year age difference naturally kept some distance between them. Declan didn't really want to hang out with his little brother all the time. They were members of the Cairns pack, but neither of them had made many friends.

Tommy had really connected with two guys his own age. Declan, however, hadn't managed to hit it off with a single person. Declan never felt very comfortable around other people. He always worried he would say something stupid and end up embarrassing himself, so most of the time he didn't say anything at all and just kept to himself. Being a pastry chef wasn't conducive to gaining friends. Declan woke up at four most mornings and crawled back into bed by no later than nine at night.

Since their parents' deaths a couple of years ago, Declan had watched over Tommy. They had packed up their lives last year and moved to Cairns, Queensland. Coming from the sweltering heat of central Australia, it seemed the perfect place. Declan hadn't really wanted to move halfway across the country, but he had to go where he could find work.

Now he just had to stick it out at his current job for

another year or so, until he'd saved up enough cash to open his own bakery. As much as he loved what he did for a living, he didn't really enjoy the job he had at the moment. It was much too commercial for his liking. He didn't want anything huge, just a small little bakery, and he thought with Cairns' large tourist population, it would suit his needs. Declan had started to count down the days until he could realise the dream he'd had since he'd been a little boy.

Pulling his phone from his pocket, Declan dialled his brother.

"'ello." The voice of his younger brother came through the phone.

"Hey, bro."

"Dec, where are you, man? I expected you home hours ago." Tommy sounded worried, and Declan really hadn't wanted that.

"Sorry, Tommy, got caught up at work. They had two staff call in sick, and I had to stay back to make sure everything got done. I'm just out at the pack grounds. I need a run. I should be home in about an hour," Declan told his brother.

"Okay, no worries. Chase, Jackson, and I will save you some pizza."

"Hah."

"Yeah, like there's going to be any left when you get through with it," Declan heard Chase say clearly through the phone line due to his enhanced hearing.

Declan laughed. His brother's friends were right; the way those boys ate food, it would be a miracle if any survived for him.

"Don't stress about it, Tommy, I can get my own food. Enjoy your evening with the guys and I'll see you soon."

"Will do. Later." Tommy hung up the phone. Declan checked to make sure the call had been disconnected, then stored his phone and his wallet in the glove compartment of his car before getting out.

Sighing, Declan glanced around, making sure no one could see him, and then he stripped his clothes and stashed them on the passenger seat. It had been forever since he'd had an opportunity to change and let his wolf run free. Yes, he and Tommy had joined the local pack, but Declan really didn't like the Alpha. The man really epitomized the word sleaze, with a capital S. Declan had yet to attend a meeting where the Alpha hadn't been leering at or trying—unsuccessfully most times—to get into the pants of most of the pack members. He didn't seem to care what gender they were or if they were already in a relationship. After the Alpha's first attempt at Declan, which he shot down, he did his best to avoid pack meetings.

He shivered in the cold night air before taking a deep breath; Declan relaxed his body and let the change come over him. Once complete, Declan shook his entire body, from snout to the tip of his tail. *God it feels good to once again be on all fours*. Lifting his muzzle slightly, he sniffed the air. Catching the scent of a nice juicy rabbit in the distance, Declan took off through the trees.

He'd been running for maybe twenty minutes when he finally got sick of playing with his food and pounced. He didn't always hunt and eat when in his wolf form, but it had been a while, and he could feel his wolf getting antsy. Hunting always calmed his other half down.

Happily chomping down his small feast, it took Declan a minute to realise what the sounds were that drifted through the trees. Taking one last bite, Declan cautiously got up from where he had been lying on the ground and slowly made his way towards the angry voices.

Step after careful step, Declan didn't want to make any noise and alert whoever to his presence. Crouching down low behind a shrub, Declan could see through into a clearing on the other side. He had thought he would be alone out here, not only because it was a Saturday night and people usually had something better to do, but also because he hadn't seen any other vehicles in the car park. There were two lots and he hadn't bothered to drive around to the other one because it surrounded the entrance all the way on the other side of the pack lands.

The angry voice of his Alpha brought his attention back to the group of men in the middle of the clearing.

"How dare you steal from me?" Alpha Kegan Wallis's hard, icy tone caused the fur on the back of

Declan's neck to stand on end.

Declan could finally recognise the man currently being held between the angry Alpha's two Betas, Gregory Stone and Barry Stuart. Nigel Cummings stood slumped over, and Declan believed the only reason he remained on his feet and not on the ground was due to the two Betas holding him up.

Nigel looked like shit. Declan had no idea what he'd done to piss the Alpha off so much, but whatever it had been, he was copping a beating for it. His eyes looked to be almost swollen shut, blood steadily oozed from a split lip, and his right cheek seemed to have split along his cheekbone.

"I didn't take anything. I swear, Alpha."

"Liar!" Declan watched Kegan Wallis punch Nigel in the stomach. Nigel doubled over, the air expelling from his lungs before the two men holding his arms roughly grabbed him and pulled him back upright.

"Do you have any idea how much a kilo of coke is worth on the Australian market?" Alpha Wallis snarled at the bruised and battered man.

"No, sir, I don't do drugs," Nigel pleaded.

Alpha Wallis sneered. "You cost me upwards of a hundred grand. All because you wanted to be cool and fit in with some fucking humans."

"I didn't, I swear. I don't do drugs. Please," Nigel begged, struggling against the men holding him.

Declan wouldn't have thought Nigel the type to steal

or try to impress what sounded like a bunch of drug-fucked humans if they wanted a kilo of coke.

Declan watched in utter horror when his Alpha pulled out a gun and pointed it at Nigel. "You really shouldn't have fucked with me, Nigel."

"No, please, it wasn't me. You have to believe m—"

Alpha Wallis cut Nigel off in the middle of his struggles when he put a bullet through his head. Declan whined quietly and quickly backed up, wanting to get away as fast as possible. Unfortunately his back leg came down on a twig and snapped it clean in half.

"What the bloody hell was that?"

Declan didn't want to hang around and find out if he had been spotted. It would be easy enough for them to know who had seen everything as soon as they caught his scent.

He took off into the forest. He had speed—probably the only thing going for him. So far, the only wolf who'd ever kept up with him had been his old Alpha, one of the fastest wolves Declan had ever met.

Declan knew the exact moment they caught his scent. Three howls ripped through the night. He didn't head back to his car. Declan kept on running. If he stopped or got caught, he would be dead before the sun crested the horizon. No way in hell would his Alpha let Declan live after he'd witnessed him killing a pack member in cold blood, let alone overheard the information his Alpha and Betas were apparently selling illegal drugs.

Declan heard them chasing him through the dense forest trees. He'd never been so scared in his life. Not when his parents had died and he'd found himself responsible for raising his younger brother or when he had packed up their lives and moved them both across the country. He started to think that particular move had been a bad idea. But seriously, who would have guessed his new Alpha would turn out to be a drug-dealing murderer? Declan wouldn't have.

Declan raced through the trees, his heart pumping, the adrenaline flowing, and he could only think about being caught and never getting to see his brother grow into the man Declan knew he could be. Tommy currently walked the fine line between teenager and responsible adult at the tender age of nineteen. Declan wanted to witness his brother's journey into manhood.

Would anyone tell Tommy what happened? Or would he go the rest of his life without being aware. Would he believe his brother dead or would he think Declan had abandoned him? Declan didn't know which option would be worse.

Silently vowing neither of those things would happen, Declan put on another burst of speed and ran.

He had no idea how long he'd journeyed, but it had to have been several hours. The sounds of pursuit were distant, but still there. He stopped for a moment to rest and catch his breath. Listening intently, he could just make out the echoes of those following him. It sounded like there were only two of them now. More than likely the Alpha had sent his Betas to do his dirty work. Kegan Wallis wouldn't want to be involved in a long, drawn-out chase through the forest. Plus, he had to get back. What would the pack say if the Alpha and both Betas suddenly disappeared?

Deciding two should be easier than three to outrun, Declan took off again. He had no idea in which direction he headed. He hadn't had a great deal of time to visit the area surrounding Cairns so didn't know any of the landmarks, not that he had come across any yet.

Declan stopped every time he found a stream of water, not only to drink, but he also walked through or swam across the cool water in hopes of losing those following him.

The sun had risen and resided high in the sky, meaning he had been running all night and well into the next day. Declan lost count of the number of streams and rivers he had crossed in the forest-covered hills. He stopped hearing sounds of pursuit some time ago, but wouldn't stop and rest in case Gregory and Barry were still on his tail. He hoped he'd lost them but didn't want to risk it just yet, so he trudged on.

Fatigue barrelled through him, the adrenaline long since gone. He was exhausted and hungry, his paws hurt from travelling for so long and not being able to rest properly, and even with his thick fur coat the constant in-

and-out of frigid waterways made him cold. He hadn't had a chance to dry completely, which caused the numbing temperature to seep into his skin.

Nothing compared to the concern he felt for his younger brother, though. Looking at the sky, he would guess the time to be somewhere close to noon. Tommy must be worried sick about the fact he hadn't come home yet. He hoped to Christ Alpha Wallis hadn't gone after his brother. He didn't really think it a possibility, but then again, he was batting a thousand with things he didn't think were possible lately.

Declan stopped for a short break and lapped at the chilly water in the stream. He sat and watched a couple of platypi swimming lazily, wishing he could be just as carefree at the moment. He decided it couldn't hurt to continue on for another hour or so, or at least until he got to a decent-sized town and could find out where the hell he'd ended up. Declan pushed his tired and aching body to continue forward.

The only noises Declan heard were the natural ones of a forest. Trees swayed in the breeze, their leaves rustling. The occasional bandicoot and echidna scurried about looking for food. And even the intermittent larger creatures like kangaroos moved about.

Perking up at an echo through the dense trees, Declan stood still and listened. He had never been so happy in his life to hear the steady hum of a motor and the heavy thud of tyres moving over bitumen. Once certain he could pinpoint the location the sound originated, Declan took off in that direction.

Less than five minutes later, he came to the edge of the forest and cautiously poked his head around the trees that lined the road. He wasn't stupid; he realised wolves weren't exactly native to the area. He didn't want to startle someone when they were driving at high speeds and cause an accident. Declan looked left and right down the black asphalt, but couldn't see anything in either direction. The lack of signage annoyed him greatly as he really would have loved to know how far he had travelled and where he'd ended up. Not knowing which way would lead to the closest town, Declan decided heading away from where he had been coming from would be his best bet.

Ducking fully back under the canopy of trees, Declan followed the road. The occasional car went flying past, but Declan ignored them, continuing on until he finally looked through the trees and saw a sign.

Atherton 5km

Declan breathed a sigh of relief, finally knowing his location. He honestly didn't know if it would be far enough away from Cairns to hide or if he would have to keep moving. Too exhausted to think about it, he decided he needed food and rest before he could make any decisions.

Chapter Two

Liam Anderson pulled his beat-up old truck into the driveway of his modest three-bedroom home and shut off the engine. He couldn't quite shake the odd sensation he'd had for the past year. He felt restless, as if waiting for something to happen, but he didn't know what.

As a Beta to Benjamin Taylor, the Pennaeth Alpha of Australia, Liam's life would never be described as dull. The Pennaeth Alpha not only had his own pack to run, he also oversaw all the other Alphas in the country. Ben made a great leader and the Australian packs had prospered since he'd come to the position. Liam felt privileged to count him as one of his closest friends. But Liam still felt as though a small part of him remained missing. He wanted, above all else, to find his mate.

The feeling had started about a year ago when Jake Richmond, the Beta from the Leyburn pack and his mate, Patrick Holland, the pack Alpha's brother, came to stay for a while. Their visit had been interesting to say the least, and Liam really couldn't be more pleased Jake and Rick had finally sorted out all their problems and settled down into mated bliss. Liam wanted what they had so badly he could almost taste it. He wished he could be so lucky. Liam had been searching a long time for his mate. Being one of the Betas required a great deal of travel, visiting other packs on behalf of the Alpha. He enjoyed the travel as it made it easier for him to continue his search for his mate. Liam had also been born with a rare gift. Not many wolves had additional abilities above and beyond the ones they all had of super strength, enhanced sight and hearing, immunity to disease, and a longer lifespan.

Liam could see mate threads. Every shifter he'd ever met had a distinctive strand that searched for its other half. As soon as Liam met the second half of a pair, a connection formed in his mind, letting him know who they were matched with. He would then let the person know where they could find their mate. He hadn't yet encountered anyone who hadn't been overjoyed at the prospect of finding their soul mate.

But throughout all the travelling and visiting of different packs and all the couples he had helped join together, he still hadn't met his own mate. Liam longed to have a soul-deep connection with a man. He wanted to love, to wake up and see the same pair of emerald green eyes every day for the rest of his life. He had no idea how he knew what colour eyes his mate had, but something inside told him he would be looking into deep green eyes.

Pushing his morose thoughts to the back of his mind, Liam removed the keys from the ignition, got out of his truck, and headed for the mailbox out front by the curb. He had forgotten to check it on Friday. After he removed what looked like two bills, he turned towards his front door, feeling the hair on the back of his arms stand up.

Liam looked around, but even with his enhanced sight, couldn't see anything in the gathering darkness. Lifting his head, Liam sniffed. He caught a slight, sweet scent on the air, but before anything could register in his brain, the scent drifted away.

Not noticing anything else out of the ordinary, Liam unlocked his house and went inside. He dumped his wallet, keys, and mail on the small hallway table he had situated by the front door, kicked his work boots off, and flicked a light switch on. Liam flexed his toes. He didn't know if his wolf or his human half detested shoes more, but he always felt better when he could be barefoot.

Liam headed into the kitchen. After a quick look in the fridge and not seeing anything that took his fancy, he opened the freezer. When in doubt, a nice juicy steak always did the trick. Pulling a pack of thick T-bones out of the freezer, Liam put them in the microwave to help the defrosting along.

Satisfied he had dinner under control for the time being, Liam grabbed a beer from the fridge. Bottle in hand, he headed down the hallway towards his bedroom, stripping his shirt as he went. The cool evening air hit his sweat-covered chest and caused his nipples to harden. He thought about lighting a fire to warm the place but decided to leave it until after he had checked his e-mails.

Even with the weather being cool during the day, they were still doing hot sweaty work. Feeling better when the dirty material had been removed from his skin, Liam threw the dirty clothes in his washing basket. He walked over to the small desk he'd set up in the corner of his room with his laptop.

Booting up the computer, Liam settled back and took a long swig of his ice-cold beer. A wolf shifter's body always ran a little hotter than a human's, and the cold beverage felt wonderful going down after a hard day at work. So much so that he didn't mind waiting for the computer to load all the start-up programs.

* * * * *

Declan felt confident he had managed to outrun the two Betas chasing him, so hopefully no one from his old pack knew of his whereabouts. He needed to contact his brother and let him know he was okay and it might be a while before he could return. Honestly, he had to admit to being a little worried about Tommy. Declan really hoped Alpha Wallis would leave his brother alone. Surely the man had to realise Declan couldn't have told his brother about what he had witnessed.

Once he'd finally made it to the town of Atherton, Declan had no idea what he should do next. Breathing deeply, the most amazing scent he'd ever smelled filled his nose and lungs, even better than fresh-baked bread or cinnamon rolls just out of the oven. His stomach rumbled violently at the thought of food. The faint smell drifted on the breeze, barely there at all, but something about it registered deep down inside Declan.

Deciding to follow his nose and see where it would lead him, Declan took off in the direction the scent originated. By the time he reached the house the aroma seemed strongest at, the waning sun had set and the temperature that had been cool to begin with dropped even lower.

Looking around to make sure no one was watching the trees behind the houses, Declan shifted, shivering as the cold night air hit the sweat currently beading on his body. Not wanting anyone to see a naked man walk across the cleared area between the houses and the tree line, Declan sprinted towards the high fence. Once safely ensconced in the dark shadows of the fence, Declan quietly and slowly opened the single gate, trying not to make any noise and alert anyone to his presence. He felt a little like a burglar on his way to complete a job, although he doubted a thief would be naked. Closing the gate just as quietly as he had opened it, Declan studied the house in front of him.

He saw lights on inside but no one walking about. The home looked like a fairly standard size for the area, from what he'd seen on his way here. It was nothing too ostentatious or flashy, just a standard single-story brick house with curtains in the windows and a garden out back. At one end of the large patio sat an outdoor setting and a barbeque and at the other end stood a pool table. A fridge completed the outdoor furniture.

Declan smiled. It looked like whoever lived here certainly knew how to entertain. He couldn't think of anything better than grilling a couple of steaks and drinking beer while playing pool and hanging out with friends. Declan lost his smile when he realised he didn't have any friends he could ever do that with. Tommy was the only constant person in his life. Declan yearned for a man he could count on, someone to share his life with.

* * * * *

The computer dinged when it had loaded and Liam opened his e-mail. He wasn't expecting much. His parents lived on the other side of town and most of his friends or pack members called if they had any problems. However, he did get e-mails for work and always checked when he got home in case something important came through.

Waiting for the damn send/receive to run, Liam took another swig of his beer. Tapping his nails on the desk, he grunted when a small chime finally sounded, letting him know his messages had arrived. He finally had a reply from a supplier about some granite he needed for an upcoming project. Liam loved his job in construction. He got to help build people's dream houses for a living. He loved the look of joy on their faces when a job had been completed.

There were drawbacks with being the boss, though. He didn't always get weekends off. Due to his work for Ben, Liam constantly found himself at a building site on a Saturday or Sunday just to give his managers a break. He didn't know what he'd do if he didn't have Miles and Aaron running things when he had to be away. The good thing about the pair being pack meant he didn't constantly have to make up excuses as to why he travelled so often. Today being Sunday, Liam had had to go to one of his sites to complete a couple of jobs that needed to be finished prior to work starting tomorrow.

Turning his attention back to his e-mail, Liam skimmed through and deleted any penis enlargement or Viagra sales, then sent the two work related e-mails to the printer before clicking on the last one.

He smiled wide when he realised the message came from Rick Holland.

> *Hey man,*
> *How are things all the way up there in sunny Queensland?*

Sunny Queensland? Liam snorted. Not likely. This time of year it was more damp, overcast, and cold than sunny.

> ***We've had nothing but rain for a fortnight now, and frankly living in a house of***

> *testosterone-filled werewolves who are stuck indoors because they don't want to get their fur wet is driving me insane. I swear I'm about two seconds away from committing a double murder. I can't quite decide which of my brothers to off first. So for the time being they all get to live. LOL*

Liam laughed at Rick's comment. He'd never met any of Rick's siblings, but he had met Rick and the man was something else. He'd held out hope for ten years his mate would finally get his head out of his ass and claim him. But he didn't do it quietly, sitting on the sidelines. Liam smiled when he remembered Jake's reaction when Liam had brought Rick home after their *date*. The man had been livid. If he remembered correctly, only a matter of days after that incident, Jake finally claimed the man he loved. Liam shook his head, trying to get his thoughts away from mates, and continued to read.

> *Although I'm not quite sure if it's the weather, my brothers, or my hormones that are making me so damn irritable lately. You know the reason we visited you last year? Yeah, well, it turns out Jake and I weren't paying as close attention to the calendar as we should have been and sort of jumped one another on a day we shouldn't have. So now, according to the doc, we'll be adding*

another to the family.

Holy fuck. Rick was pregnant!

I'm over the moon. Always wanted kids but just assumed it would never happen. Jake, on the other hand, is a little freaked. I think he's worried about turning out like his father. When he's not flipping out about becoming a dad, he's hovering, making sure I'm okay. He jumps at the slightest move I make and I reckon, if I let him, he would carry me everywhere until this was all over.

Liam understood Jake's worries. The man's father had been a homophobic asshole who had kept them apart for ten years by threatening to have Rick killed if Jake so much as touched the man. He had even gone so far as to try and shoot both when they had been out running on the full moon soon after they returned home from Atherton. Ben had been informed about what had taken place and Rick had sent Liam an e-mail soon after, filling in all the missing details.

Mum and Dad can't wait. Mum's in her element, surrounded by grandkids. Me, I can't stop eating. I'm hungry all the damn time and for the weirdest shit. At the moment I can't seem to get enough of marshmallows and balsamic

> *vinegar. (Not together, thank God.) I constantly have to send Jake to the shop because we keep running out. God, I'm gonna be the size of a house soon. LOL. Oh well, all I can say is thank God for a high metabolism.*

Marshmallows and balsamic vinegar? Eww. No way could Liam handle all that sugar, let alone the acid in the vinegar in the amounts Rick seemed to be consuming. He hoped Rick ate the balsamic with something, like bread or salad, and didn't drink it straight from the bottle.

Liam had never really thought about having children. He figured there wouldn't be a point longing for something that wouldn't happen unless he somehow did the impossible and found his mate. So he didn't allow himself to think about it.

> *Anyway, I think I've rambled on for long enough, plus I'm pretty sure I can hear Jake coming down the hallway, probably wondering if I need anything. I love that man more than my life, but sometimes he can be a bit overbearing. So I'm going to sign off now and go deal with my very overprotective mate. I hope everything is well with yourself and Ben.*
>
> *In friendship,*
> *Rick Holland*

The microwave beeped at the same moment Liam's stomach rumbled, sounding like it would give a good try at eating its way out of his body. Deciding to deal with dinner first, Liam put the lid down on his laptop and headed back to the kitchen down the hallway. He would reply to Rick's e-mail after he had eaten and thought about how he would congratulate the happy couple.

Nothing much had changed in Liam's life since Rick and Jake had left. He had no significant other to write about; hell, there had only been a handful of one-night stands in the past year. Even with his business doing well, he didn't think Rick would be interested in hearing about the ups and downs of building houses in Atherton and the surrounding areas.

* * * * *

Movement in the house startled Declan and he watched as a man made his way into the kitchen. *Yum.* He moved closer to get a better look. Declan had never thought of himself as short, but compared to the man who just walked in, he started thinking it. The stunning specimen had probably four or five inches on Declan's own five foot eleven. His dirty blond hair had a little length on top.

The fact the man wore no shirt caught Declan's attention and held it. Declan wanted to feel those stunning muscles rippling under his fingers. What had

Declan drooling most of all was the large tattoo. It covered his entire right arm, his right pectoral muscle, and when he turned around, Declan could see it also covered his right shoulder. The entire tattoo had been created in nothing but black ink; however, it still managed to look like flames licking their way up the man's arm and across his body.

Declan's mouth watered at the thought of running his tongue along every single inch of the black design. Being otherwise occupied fixating on the tattoo, he hadn't been paying attention to what he was doing. Without realising it, he'd walked right up to the kitchen window.

* * * * *

Liam pulled the steaks out of the microwave and left them on the bench for a minute while he grabbed a couple of potatoes out of the cupboard. He turned around to grab a fork to stab the spuds with and nearly had a heart attack.

Outside his kitchen window stood a man.

Liam's heart pounded so fast he thought it would explode. His right hand came up and pressed against his chest. He could feel the frantic thumping under his fingers. Liam took a deep breath and tried to calm his body.

* * * * *

Declan couldn't take his eyes off the man. Yes, he looked a little pale from finding someone standing outside his kitchen. Those big silver eyes, however, held warmth that Declan just wanted to curl up into.

Declan watched in quiet fascination as the man covered his heart with his hand as if he could force the thing to once again beat at a normal rhythm. The man's pulse pounded in his neck. Declan had no idea how long they stood there staring at one another. Declan couldn't have broken the eye contact with the stunning man if his life depended on it.

His body, however, wasn't in complete sync with the rest of him, and he shuddered and shook from the cold. He'd been standing still for far too long, and the chill had completely seeped under his skin down to his bones. Declan wrapped his arms around his middle, watching the man walk towards the back door.

* * * * *

Back in control, Liam gathered all his wits and concentrated on his visitor. How had he come to be standing there? That was just one of many questions Liam wanted answered. Gazing outside, Liam took in details he hadn't seen when he originally spotted him.

The pitch-black night hadn't made making out

particulars easy, but the kitchen light helped Liam see the imploring look in the man's eyes. He appeared to be exhausted and breathing fairly heavily, if the rise and fall of his chest was anything to go by. The man's dark hair stuck to his head, probably with sweat.

And he shivered. Liam's gaze travelled down from the man's face and landed on a naked torso. The guy had to be freezing, standing out in the cool night air covered in perspiration.

* * * * *

Apart from freezing to death from standing out on the back patio, Declan would have one other disadvantage if the man stepped outside. The guy would find a naked, fully aroused male.

Declan had a sudden moment of insight. Could this man be the source of the incredible aroma? He had no control over the state he currently found his own body in, an almost unconscious reaction to the alluring scent he had been following. The wonderful smell permeated the air, causing Declan's body to positively hum with want and arousal. He had an idea what it meant, what would happen when the door opened.

The man in the kitchen was a complete stranger. Declan knew absolutely nothing about him. Hell, he didn't even know if someone else he'd yet to see would soon be joining them. Would the man be homophobic and turn abusive at the first sight of Declan's condition? He sure hoped not. The guy didn't look like the type to use his fists against those that were smaller than him, but Declan didn't really know. Would the sexy stud be gay or straight? God, Declan really hoped for gay, even though the odds were slim. Whatever happened, it would have to be one of the most awkward first meetings of Declan's life.

* * * * *

Liam made his way slowly to the back door, never once taking his eyes from the man standing outside his window. Flicking the switch to operate the lights on the back patio, Liam opened the door. Stepping outside, he inhaled sharply with surprise when he found the man completely naked, his arms wrapped around his waist from the cold. It didn't escape his notice however, how gorgeous the other man looked.

* * * * *

Declan blinked rapidly when the lights suddenly shone down on him. He never would have thought he would be introducing himself to a complete stranger while standing outside his back door completely naked, aroused, and freezing.

Declan took a step back when the man exited his

home and joined him on the back porch. He sucked in a harsh breath at the stabbing pins and needles when his legs protested the move. Declan stood in silence, not sure what to say. He met the stranger's gaze and felt a jolt arc through his body, making its way directly to his cock, which bobbed happily despite the cold.

The man in front of him seemed to collapse a little before he caught himself.

* * * * *

A gentle breeze brought the scent of earth and man with a hint of something sweet. Liam's eyes widened when he realised he'd smelt that particular scent earlier. His cock stood up and took notice immediately. Liam's gums ached when his canines threatened to descend. As soon as his eyes made contact with the stranger's, he noticed the mate thread, bright and golden, reaching out to him, wanting to join with his own.

Liam staggered and reached out for the doorframe to help him stay upright when the meaning of what had just happened registered in his brain.

He had finally met his mate.

<u>Chapter Three</u>

A broad grin spread across the man's face as he straightened to his full height. "Please, come in, you must be freezing. It's got to be close to ten degrees out here."

His deep, rich voice slid over Declan's skin like warm melted chocolate, even if it did waver slightly. That surprised Declan. Why would this man be nervous?

He watched as the blond god opened the door wider and stood to the side, allowing Declan entrance into his house. Declan usually didn't enter strangers' houses naked, but after what he had been through over the last twenty-four hours, he'd take a chance. Plus, anyone who smelled that good couldn't be a bad person. Right? Declan tried to convince himself as he slowly walked forward.

His muscles protested their use, but he took it slowly. As he got closer to the man, the scent that had been tormenting him all day became even stronger. Declan wanted to surround himself in it and roll around on the floor until completely covered. His cock throbbed again, and not until he had taken his first steps into the house did his cold-addled brain finally catch up with his body and he realise exactly what it all meant.

He turned around sharply, gasping, and stared at the other man. *His mate*. The incredibly appealing man still standing in the back doorway was his mate.

* * * * *

Liam's head reeled. He never thought this day would come, especially not on a cold night in his backyard. He wondered what had caused his mate to turn up at his house naked as the day he had been born. Liam figured something had happened, and he'd been forced to shift. The one downside to changing form? Complete nakedness before and after shifting. Better, however, than leaving a large pile of rags as the realigning of limbs tended to rip clothing seams. Stripping down saved getting caught up in the remnants.

Realising he'd been standing in the doorway gazing at the other man for far too long, Liam shook his head to get his brain back into working order.

Closing the door, he moved past the man. "Would you like a shower? I think the warmth will do you some good." Liam hadn't gotten around to starting a fire in his little potbelly stove yet; now he wished he had.

As soon as he saw to his mate, he would get right on it. The man had started to turn a bluish purple in places. Being out in the weather naked hadn't been good for him.

His mate blushed and another shiver racked his body. "Thank you. That would be great."

Liam's heart skipped a beat at the first sound of his mate's voice. The light, almost musical sound made him think of warm honey.

"I'm Liam Anderson, by the way, and this is my home." He really wanted to know his mate's name and thought if he introduced himself, it might entice the man to follow suit.

"Declan Morgan," his mate said with a slight smile.

"Declan. Morgan." Liam would be happy to stand there and repeat that name all day.

He would never tire of saying or hearing Declan's name. "It's a great pleasure to finally meet you. Come with me and I'll show you to the bathroom. I'll get you some sweats and a shirt for you to put on when you're finished."

"Thank you," Declan replied softly, tight lines of exhaustion marring his beautiful face.

Liam's cock throbbed painfully within the tight confines of his jeans, but he made his way out of the kitchen and into the hallway, making sure Declan followed. He paused and grabbed a clean towel out of the linen press and opened the door to the bathroom.

"Help yourself to anything you need. I'll be back in a sec with some warm clothes." Liam put the towel on the rack and exited the bathroom before he did something inappropriate like shove his sexy mate up against the wall and plunder his mouth as if his life depended on it.

Liam walked to the end of the hallway and into his room. He collapsed onto his bed, bringing his right arm up to cover his eyes, moving his left hand down to thump his raging erection. He needed to control his rampant libido. Declan had obviously been running from something, otherwise they would have met like every other couple—fully clothed.

When Liam finally regained control of his body and his cock had softened sufficiently, he rose from the bed and searched through his closet for something that would fit the smaller man. Not finding anything, he settled for a pair of his sweats with a drawstring and one of his long-sleeved shirts.

Heading back down the hall, he heard the shower running. Taking a deep breath to gather his nerves, Liam knocked once, then opened the door. All the air rushed from his lungs when he saw the silhouette of his naked mate standing under the running water. The glass shower door did absolutely nothing to hide his appearance.

"Here are some clothes." Liam couldn't help the fact that his voice deepened. He placed the clothes on the counter next to the sink and bolted from the room before he could strip and join his mate.

He heard a muffled 'thank you' as he quickly closed the door. In his living room, Liam pulled himself together and started a fire in the potbelly stove before he headed back into the kitchen to get dinner started. He'd bet his mate had to be hungry, and Liam's stomach rumbled, reminding him he hadn't eaten either.

Stabbing some extra potatoes, he put them in the oven to cook. From the fridge, he pulled out some carrots and cabbage, and grabbed a red onion from the pantry. Halfway through grating the carrot, Liam felt the air shift around him and the smell of his mate mingled with soap drifted to him.

He turned around to find Declan standing in the doorway looking shy and unsure.

Liam stopped and wiped his hands on a dish towel before walking over to face his mate. He gently caressed Declan's cheek with his fingertips.

"Do you know who I am?" he whispered.

Declan's eyes closed and he nodded.

Liam didn't miss the slightly haunted look in his mate's gaze.

Liam leant forward and placed a gentle chaste kiss on his mate's lips before stepping back. "I'm not sure what's happened or what you're running from, but I will never hurt you."

Declan gave him a jerky nod, and Liam changed the subject. "Now, is there anything you need before dinner? You can go and sit in the living room and warm up in front of the fire for a while if you'd like."

Declan seemed to hesitate for a minute before finally talking. "Um, could I—um, possibly use your, um, phone. I have to call my brother."

His man looked so sweet standing there acting so unsure of himself.

"Of course. You can have anything you want." Liam reached into his pocket and grabbed his phone. "The PIN number is one three zero eight."

Declan's eyes went wide for a moment before he reached out and took the phone. Liam had no idea where the number came from but when he needed to enter a PIN on his first bank account, those four digits stuck in his head. He used the sequence for everything now. It probably wasn't smart of him, but he couldn't seem to bring himself to stop using them.

"Why don't you go into the living room where it's nice and warm and give your brother a call? Dinner should be ready in about fifteen minutes. It's nothing special, just some steak, a baked potato, and some coleslaw," Liam said as he pointed the way to the living room.

Declan nodded and turned to leave the kitchen. He paused in the doorway and looked back. "Thank you."

Liam sighed. He could already tell it would be a fight to keep his hands off Declan. He licked his lips, trying to gather any remaining taste of his mate that might still be lingering after the brief but wonderful kiss Liam had taken earlier.

He chuckled and got back to dinner. No matter how big or strong the wolf, they always seemed to turn to jelly as soon as a mate came into the picture. Jake Richmond from the Leyburn pack proved that last year when he visited with Rick. Now Liam figured his turn had come to follow in every other wolf's steps. He looked forward to it.

Smiling, Liam got to work; he heated the inside grill pan and put the steaks on to cook before he finished making the coleslaw.

<u>Chapter Four</u>

Declan collapsed on the couch, overwhelmed by everything that had happened to him in the last twenty-four hours. The large deep-mahogany leather sofa nearly swallowed him whole. The fire in the corner filled the room with its warmth. Declan snuggled down into the luxurious couch, pulling the blanket from the back and covering himself.

Sighing deeply, he lifted the phone in his hand, a little rattled Liam had used his birthdate as his password. At least he wouldn't likely forget it. Unlocking the phone, he dialled his brother's number.

The line on the other end had barely even rung once before Tommy picked up.

"Hello?" His brother's voice sounded so good.

"Tommy," Declan barely got out around the lump in his throat. He needed to get himself together.

"Dec? Oh my God, where the hell are you? No one seems to know where you disappeared to." His younger brother sounded slightly hysterical.

"Hey, kid, I'm okay. Please try and calm down. Are you there by yourself?" He desperately needed to know if the Alpha had tried to contact his brother.

"Chase and Jackson are here with me. Bro, what the hell's going on? Why did you take off like that?" Tommy asked, worry clearly evident in his voice. His brother paused a moment before continuing "And I hate to be the bearer of bad news, but after not rocking up to work today and no notification, they called earlier and said not to bother coming back."

Declan cringed, although he shouldn't have been surprised. He didn't really like his job anyway. He had been working in a factory-type setting, making large amounts of the same recipes so they could be delivered to various cafés and restaurants. Declan much preferred the smaller, more intimate feeling a bakery offered. Could be why he dreamed of owning and operating his own place.

Now with no job, he'd be hard-pressed to earn the money he needed to realise his goal. But first he had to deal with the fact he'd been chased by his deranged, drug-dealing, murderous Alpha and his two Betas for witnessing them kill Nigel.

"Declan?" Tommy sounded concerned again.

Shit. He had to get his head on straight and talk to his brother. He didn't want to cause any further worry.

"Yeah, I'm here, sorry. Was just thinking." Declan steadied his nerves before he continued. "Listen, kid, I need you to do something for me, okay?"

"Whatever you need, you know that." No hesitation, even after everything. Declan really loved his brother.

"Yeah, I need you to lay low for a while. Please don't ask me why, it's probably best if you don't know. And please promise me if you see Alpha Wallis or either of his Betas, you'll run, get out of the house and go somewhere safe." He had to be scaring the crap out of his brother, but he didn't know what else to do. He needed Tommy safe.

"What the fuck's going on, Declan?" Apprehension filled Tommy's voice.

He wished he could do more to reassure Tommy. God, why the hell did he decide to take a run after getting off work? Why couldn't he have just gone home like every other Goddamned night?

"I'm sorry, Tommy, but I need you to promise me. Run if you see the Alpha or the Betas. Please." Declan would do anything if it meant keeping his brother safe.

"Okay, Dec. If I see them, I'll hightail it out of here and head over to Chase's place. Now where are you?"

Declan hesitated. He really didn't want to say anything that could cause any problems for his brother. "It's not important," he finally answered. He quickly added, "But in all this shit there is a silver lining—well, at least I think there is." Declan thought of Liam and hoped to Christ he was a good thing. He hoped to distract Tommy from the fact he didn't answer his question satisfactorily.

"What do you mean it's not important? And what silver lining? I've been going out of my freaking mind with worry over you."

Declan cringed. Tommy would've been worried when he hadn't made it home last night.

"I know, and I'm sorry it's not entirely safe for me to

tell you where I am." Tommy couldn't tell others what he didn't know. "And the good news, I met my mate tonight."

"What?" Tommy screeched over the phone, all traces of fear gone. "Seriously, dude? What's he like? Is he hot? Oh God, please tell me it's a he?"

Declan had sat his kid brother down years ago and told him about his sexuality. They'd had a long talk about being gay and what it meant. Their parents had been accepting of his sexuality, and his brother proved no different.

Declan laughed for the first time in days. "Yes, it's a guy. And holy Jesus, Mary, and Joseph, is he hot. All big and strong with muscles that just won't quit and this tattoo I just want to lick. With everything else going on, the timing sucks, but I don't really care."

"Sounds nice, Declan. You know as well as I do that everything happens for a reason. Take a chance, bro. You've been alone for far too long." Tommy sounded genuinely happy.

Declan sighed. He had some thinking to do but felt too exhausted to focus on anything. His stomach chose that moment to let it be known it wanted food. He felt dead on his feet and really didn't want to move. He needed rest.

"I know. Hey, I have to go. I need some sleep. I'll call you in a couple of days to check on you. Could you have one of your friends head to the pack grounds and check if my car's still there? It should have my wallet, phone, and keys in it." He hoped no one had stolen it.

"Yeah, will do. Get some rest and enjoy your mate. I'll talk to you soon. Love ya, Dec," Tommy said.

"Thanks. I love you too, Tommy." Declan hung up the phone and sighed.

* * * * *

Liam hoped someday Declan loved him as much as he obviously cared about his brother. Declan lay curled up on his couch, covered from his feet right up to the base of his neck by Liam's favourite blanket. The only parts of Declan peeking from under the blanket were his head and the fingers of his hand as he held the phone to his ear.

Liam had to bite his tongue when he walked in to hear Declan describe him to his brother. He didn't know whether to laugh or stalk across the room and kiss the man until their lungs burned from lack of oxygen.

Instead he'd waited patiently for Declan to finish his conversation. He didn't want to embarrass the other man by letting him know he'd been overheard.

Liam cleared his throat and rapped twice on the wall, hoping he would get Declan's attention. Declan started slightly and tried to cover it by sitting up, but Liam still saw it. He'd hoped to make enough noise that he wouldn't startle Declan.

"Dinner's ready," he announced casually.

"Thank you. I'll be right there." Declan's voice sounded barely more than a whisper.

"Take your time." Liam offered a friendly smile before turning and heading back into the kitchen.

Liam plated up the food and placed it on the table before going back for drinks and cutlery. Grabbing two beers from the fridge, he set them on the table and sat down. He only had to wait a moment before Declan slowly walked in and sat opposite him.

"Thank you," he said again quietly.

"You're welcome. Now eat up. You look dead on your feet." Liam cut into his steak.

Declan quietly chuckled. "I'm so tired I can barely lift my knife and fork, but I'll force myself because this smells amazing and I'm starving."

"It's nothing special. I'll show you to the guest room as soon as we're done here."

Declan nodded in understanding but seemed too intent on his food at the moment to converse further. Liam took a long drink of his beer, trying to cool his awareness of the other wolf, before he turned back and concentrated on eating his food. Before he knew it, they were both finished with dinner, and Declan's eyes were drooping. Liam picked up Declan's plate and his own and took them back into the kitchen and placed them in the sink. He'd worry about cleaning them after he settled his mate down for the night.

His mate! Liam still found it a little hard to believe he had finally met the man fated to be his, let alone the fact he had just rocked up on his doorstep completely naked. Liam shook his head to dislodge the thoughts and images. He would be hard as stone if he kept thinking about what Declan looked like under his clothes.

After several moments of willing his body not to betray him, Liam got himself under control and walked back into the dining area. Declan remained at the table, holding his half-finished beer. He looked so tired Liam thought he might fall asleep where he sat.

"Come on, Declan, let's get you tucked into bed. I don't think either of us is ready for me to be getting in there with you, as much as I would love to, some other time soon, maybe?"

Liam helped Declan stand, and the smaller man turned into his side and seemed to snuggle in. Liam felt the soft laugh vibrate against his body.

"Yeah, definitely some other time," Declan said.

Liam held Declan close, and they made their way down the hall to the guest room nearest Liam's bedroom. Liam wouldn't sleep with his mate under the same roof, even if they were in separate rooms. If they couldn't share a bed yet, at least Declan would be as close as possible. Liam turned the light on when they entered the bedroom, and not too soon either. Declan's body had been getting heavier and heavier as they walked up the hall. Liam leant down and pulled the sheets back on the bed before manoeuvring Declan to sit down on the side.

Liam reached down and grabbed the hem Declan's shirt. "Up," he said quietly, not wanting to startle the nearly asleep man.

Declan's arms moved sluggishly upwards, and Liam struggled a little to remove the much too large shirt. As sexy as he found his mate in his clothes, he didn't want the man to get tangled in his sleep.

The sweats, on the other hand, he would leave. Liam threw the shirt over the tallboy at the end of the bed. Laying Declan down, he lifted his mate's legs and got them under the blankets. He then pulled the doona up until he completely covered his mate, leaving nothing showing but his head on the pillow.

Liam tucked a stray lock of hair behind Declan's ear before he bent down and placed a quick gentle kiss on Declan's lips. "Sleep well, my mate."

Declan's hand shot out from under the blankets in a surprising show of alertness, and he gripped Liam midretreat. "Thank you," he whispered and squeezed Liam's fingers once before dropping back to the bed.

A little snore not even ten seconds later told Liam his mate had finally succumbed to his exhaustion. Liam couldn't help it, he stood and watched the other man sleeping for several minutes, still awed and amazed by Declan's appearance in his life.

He couldn't stand watch over Declan like a predator stalking his prey all night. Liam headed back to the dining room and kitchen to clean up the dinner dishes. After the excitement of the day, Liam was too keyed up to be able to relax just yet, so he finished putting everything away, pulled another beer from the fridge and headed for the living room.

He sat on the couch where Declan had been lying earlier and pulled the rumpled blanket to his nose. The sweet scent of his mate still lingered in the fibres, and Liam sighed in happiness. Something must have happened to Declan. Why else would he show up naked on Liam's doorstep? He would wait until the other man felt comfortable enough to confide in him. It might kill him in the meantime, but whatever Declan needed, Liam would try to provide.

Chapter Five

Declan came back to consciousness slowly, confused by the unfamiliar softness of the mattress underneath him. The sheets were wrong, a much higher quality than his own cheaply bought Kmart ones.

He blinked at the bright light shining through the curtains, becoming more alert. Declan had a brief moment of panic he'd be late for work but calmed down when something niggled at the back of his brain telling him everything would be okay. He hadn't slept so late in years; he usually woke up well before the sun rose, even on his rare days off.

He looked around the room, positive he'd never stepped foot in it before. It was fairly sparse and furnished with just the large queen-sized bed, a set of bedside drawers with two lamps on top, and a tallboy against the wall opposite the bed.

It looked like a typical guest room for someone who didn't get a great deal of visitors. Declan sat up slowly, the sheets pooling around his waist. Surprised to be naked down to his waist, Declan quickly lifted the covers. He sighed in relief, glad to be wearing sweats. He honestly didn't remember getting to bed last night or getting undressed.

A knock on the bedroom door startled Declan. He breathed in deeply trying to get the scent of the person on the other side. The aroma seeped into his body, filling every pore and causing such a visceral reaction that memory came flooding back. Liam. *His mate.*

Declan thumped his hand down on his hard cock, not wanting the bulge beneath the blankets to be obvious.

After attempting to talk and having no sound come out, he cleared his throat. "Come in." He really needed his morning coffee.

Declan watched as Liam opened the door and stepped inside the room. His eyes swept over every inch of Declan's naked skin before making their way to meet his eyes. Declan smiled shyly when their gazes connected. Declan didn't know what to do with the undisguised heat that shone out of Liam's stunning eyes. No one had ever looked at him like that before.

"Morning," Liam said.

Declan didn't think it was his imagination that Liam's voice sounded deeper than it did last night.

"Good morning," Declan replied, silently begging his heart to stop trying to beat its way out of his chest.

His wolf sat up and took notice. The creature wanted to reach out and touch its mate; Declan held back, barely, from giving in to its wants.

"There's coffee if you're interested," Liam said, his voice still low and sexy as hell.

"Oh yeah!" Declan exclaimed and jumped out of bed.

Liam chuckled but Declan didn't care. His day didn't start right if it didn't begin with caffeine. Being a baker and having to get up at unimaginable hours of the morning, coffee had fast become a necessity in his life.

Declan headed out of the room, wearing nothing but his sweats. Pausing for a moment when he passed Liam, he raised up so he could lay a quick, gentle kiss on Liam's cheek. "Thank you," he said quietly, unable, after all, to pass his mate without touching.

"You're welcome." Liam smiled. "I don't know for what, but you're welcome anyway."

His sweet smile turned into a cheeky grin and Declan laughed.

Liam followed him through the house to the kitchen. Declan didn't stop, and even though the house didn't belong to him, he headed directly for the coffee maker sitting on the bench. Declan looked in three cupboards before he found the coffee mugs. He didn't have to search for the coffee; the pods were hanging on the wall directly behind the coffee maker.

Declan had no worries working the DeLonghi Nespresso machine; he had one just like it at home. The milk had been topped up, and Declan placed his cup under the spout, then looked at the different varieties of coffee pods. Letting out a very unmanly squeal when he saw his favourite flavour, he quickly reached out and pulled the pod from its box and placed it in the machine. He closed the lid, pressed the buttons, and waited.

The machine whirred to life, and Declan bounced on the balls of his feet, impatient for the damn thing to finish. The rich smell drove him crazy. He wished it would hurry up already; he wanted his coffee now! When the cappuccino finally finished, Declan grabbed the chocolate shaker sitting next to the machine and sprinkled a generous amount on top of the foamy milk.

Picking up the cup, Declan took his first sip and sighed. Heaven. God, he loved the first coffee of the day. He took several more sips of his drink before the chuckling behind him registered. Declan turned around to find Liam leaning against the bench opposite him, his eyes filled with mirth and something Declan couldn't put a name to. The man looked drop-dead sexy when he relaxed and laughed.

"So…" Liam said.

Declan waited but Liam didn't seem to want to follow on after that one word.

"So?" Declan asked finally, not able to help himself.

"Like your coffee, do you?" Liam laughed again.

Declan blushed. He must look like a right idiot with the way he acted about a silly drink, but Declan really did like his coffee. Not wanting to say anything, he simply lifted his cup and took another sip after nodding quickly.

Liam truly did have a beautiful smile. Declan hoped that smile would always be directed towards him. At the thought, he shook his head. On the one hand, he barely knew the man; on the other, they were mates. Declan had grown up in a loving family, his parents had been a fated pairing, and he had been taught all about mates. He never imagined the bonding pull would be so strong after such little time, though.

Wanting to change the subject before he jumped the unsuspecting man, Declan blurted, "What day is it?"

Liam studied him for a moment before he answered. "It's Monday morning." He looked down at his watch and winced. "If I don't leave right now, I'm going to be late for work, and it never looks good when the boss is late." He smiled lightly.

Declan wondered what Liam did for a living. He had a feeling it included some sort of manual labour. The man looked magnificent in faded, work-roughened jeans that he thought were probably as soft as silk. Declan desperately wanted to touch and find out. The shirt Liam wore hugged his abdominals perfectly and made Declan's mouth fill with saliva at the thought of pushing it up and licking the tight muscles underneath.

An open flannel shirt with the sleeves rolled halfway up Liam's powerful arms and scuffed steel-toed boots completed the outfit. Oh yeah, his mate definitely worked with his hands. Declan really wanted Liam to work him with his hands; he could just about imagine the rough, callused fingers moving over his body, bringing nothing but pleasure. Declan closed his eyes as his mind wandered. A small whimper escaped as he thought about Liam grasping his cock in his tight fist.

A strong hand in his hair gripping tightly and tilting

his head back surprised him. He hadn't even heard Liam move. He blinked his eyes open, staring up at a silver gaze that radiated heat.

"Stop it!" Liam's voice had gone low and guttural as if he struggled to keep control.

"Huh?" Declan had no idea what Liam referred to. He hadn't done anything.

"Whatever it is you're thinking, stop it now, or I won't be going to work today. I'll be bending you over every surface in this house I can find."

Declan's cock jumped and pulsed at the idea, and he tried to bite back another moan, he really did.

"Fuck, you're beautiful," Liam whispered before his lips descended in a punishing kiss that stole Declan's breath and made his heart rate elevate to dangerous levels.

Just when Declan thought he would pass out from lack of oxygen, Liam pulled back. He placed one last, gentler kiss against Declan's lips before he stepped back.

"Hang around the house today. I'll be home at four this afternoon." Liam gently swiped his thumb over Declan's swollen bottom lip. "If you need me at all, my number is by the house phone. Feel free to call your brother again if you wish."

Declan opened his mouth, wanting to suck on Liam's thumb, but Liam removed his hand entirely.

"Tonight I'll take you so you can talk with Ben, followed by poker with the guys." Liam slowly walked backwards towards the entrance to the kitchen as he spoke.

"Um, Ben? Poker?" Declan's brain still wasn't firing on all cylinders, and he had a little trouble understanding why he would want to talk to this Ben person.

"Monday night is poker night. It's the only night all the guys have off. And Ben is my Alpha. Technically he's your Alpha as well, seeing as how he's the Pennaeth Alpha of all the packs in Australia," Liam answered.

"Holy shit," Declan whispered. How the hell had he been so lucky as to end up here?

Liam laughed and waggled his brows. "Be safe, my mate. I'll see you when I get home. Oh, and keep your hands to yourself today."

Declan must have looked as confused at the last statement. Liam's gaze dropped down to the tented front of his sweats, and Declan blushed deeply.

Declan didn't say anything, and Liam raised his left brow in question. Declan's face burned but he nodded anyway. Liam shoved his wallet and phone in his pocket and picked up his keys.

"Bye." Declan stood in the kitchen still holding his now-empty coffee cup and watched Liam walk out of the room.

A few seconds later, the front door closed and a truck started. Declan released the breath he didn't realise he'd been holding and collapsed back against the kitchen bench. He needed to get it together. Was he nervous about meeting with the Pennaeth Alpha later today? Hell, yes. But that didn't even compare with the butterflies doing dive bombs in his stomach at the prospect of meeting Liam's friends for poker.

What if they didn't like him? He and Liam weren't even mated yet, hadn't done anything more than kiss. Would Liam send him away if his friends found him lacking? Declan hoped not, as he had nowhere else to go but back to an Alpha who probably wanted to kill him to keep him quiet about what the man had been up to. Hell, Declan didn't even have a job anymore. He had his brother and his mate. At least he hoped so. Surely the Pennaeth would be able to help him out of his current situation. Ben would want to know about Wallis, wouldn't he? Worrying about it wouldn't help. Declan quickly washed the few dishes in the sink from Liam's breakfast and set them aside to dry. He then decided to explore the house. Declan had a good eight hours to fill. He had no idea what he would do, but he hoped to find something.

* * * * *

Hot and sweaty and in desperate need of a shower, Liam drove home. All day his thoughts had not been on the job; instead they'd been hijacked by his handsome mate and the way Declan looked when Liam walked out of the kitchen that morning.

He had no idea what Declan had been thinking about, but Liam had been spellbound, standing there and watching Declan close his eyes, his face flushed and his sweats noticeably tented. What really caught Liam's attention, though, had been the strong scent of lust hanging heavy in the air. Liam thought it almost thick enough to choke on. He'd had to hightail it out, otherwise he would have done what he told Declan and spent the entire day fucking his mate over every surface in his house. As fun as it sounded, he didn't know if Declan would be ready for the kind of hot sex Liam craved with his mate or not. He didn't want to rush Declan into anything as he still had no idea what had caused his mate's sudden appearance on his doorstep.

Even with his mind not being focused solely on what it should have been, Liam had had a great day and managed to get a lot of work done. He didn't even yell at the men who delivered the wrong bathroom and tap supplies to three different houses. Liam was just thankful he had picked up on the mistake before they had started drilling holes in the shower tiles. It would have been a huge pain in the ass to have to re-tile part of the shower.

He knew he'd walked around all day with a stupid grin on his face. Even though Liam had yet to claim Declan, the fact he'd met his mate and had already fallen for the beautiful man made him happy beyond belief. He had even caught himself whistling a couple of times. Liam also didn't miss the curious looks from his employees when they watched him move about the various worksites.

The day finally ended and he headed back to his house and his mate. He couldn't believe how excited he felt just to get to see his Declan again. After pulling into the driveway, Liam shut off the car and walked to his front door.

The most heavenly scent surrounded Liam and hugged him close. The appealing aroma seemed to be a mixture of his mate plus chocolate and rich caramel. He loved the fact that it seemed his Declan's scent had started to permeate his home. Liam had no concerns about being heard when he closed the door as music blasted from the direction of the kitchen. He kicked his boots off and headed towards the noise.

Liam stopped in the doorway to the kitchen and caught his breath, his cock instantly perking up. Declan had Liam's iPod and docking station from his bedroom, and he'd plugged it into the wall. Currently listening to Gym Class Heroes' "The Fighter," Declan sang along with the music, his ass bopping along to the beat. Liam's chest tightened at the sight before him, and his cock hardened within its tight confines. God, the man was sexy as hell.

Declan moved and swayed while piping cream into what looked like éclair shells. Liam didn't even know he owned a piping bag. Declan placed the cream-filled pastries on a tray and covered the tops in rich melted chocolate. The kitchen, which he would have assumed to be a disaster area, at least it would have been if he had been the one cooking, was spotless.

The music changed and Nickelback's "Lullaby" came on. Declan never stopped moving or singing. Halfway through a turn, Declan noticed Liam standing in the doorway. Declan stood still, bare-chested, with pink tinting his cheeks at being caught dancing and singing and what looked like a smudge of chocolate in the corner of his mouth.

Liam prowled across the room, his eyes never straying very far from Declan's delicious-looking lips. Declan swallowed audibly when Liam rounded the kitchen bench and reached out. Wrapping his hand around the back of Declan's neck, Liam pulled the man close, leaning in and licking at the smudge along the edge of his lips. The taste of chocolate and his mate burst across Liam's tongue, and he moaned, his cock hardening further.

Lips met, tongues duelled, and Liam felt like his body would burst into flames. His dick ached in his suddenly too-tight jeans. Liam forcefully pulled back, breaking the kiss. Panting, trying to regain his breath, Liam stared at the lust-filled eyes of his mate.

"Please." The whispered word had so much want and longing, Liam would have been a fool to ignore it.

He looked down and noticed Declan still held the piping bag. He carefully removed it from his fingers and placed it on the bench.

"Will this be okay here for a little while, or do you need to put it away?" He might be horny, but he didn't want to ruin anything his mate had been working on.

Declan smiled. "Thank you. I'll leave the chocolate, but the rest really should go in the fridge."

Liam gave Declan room to quickly pack everything up. The second the fridge door closed, Liam stepped up and bent down a little. He picked Declan up and placed him over his shoulder and took off for his bedroom. To finally claim his mate, he would do it properly in a bed.

Declan laughed. "You know I could have walked?"

Liam smacked his ass. "Hush." He didn't miss Declan's moan or the way he squirmed and seemed to stick his butt out farther.

Chapter Six

Declan cried out again as Liam's large, callused hand came down once more on his behind. Who would have thought he'd like getting spanked? Certainly not him. Reaching out, Declan lifted the tail of Liam's shirt, giving himself a perfect view of Liam's ass encased in denim. He'd just reached out to cup one fine cheek when he went sailing through the air. He landed softly on Liam's bed.

Scooting back, Declan propped himself up against the pillows at the head of the bed and watched Liam make short work of the clothes he wore.

"You know you could slow down and make that a whole hell of a lot sexier," Declan stated.

Liam paused for a moment, then smiled. "Next time."

His grin turned entirely too wicked. Declan's cock grew and throbbed in the sweat pants.

Liam's muscles bunched and tightened when he lifted his shirt off over his head. Declan moaned at the sight before him. Liam stood in his jeans and socks, the afternoon light through the curtains giving him a golden glow. Declan practically salivated and wanted to run his tongue over every inch of the large tattoo covering his mate's right side.

Liam reached for the opening on his jeans, then looked up, lust shining in his eyes. "You know it usually helps if you get naked too."

Declan nodded quickly before hastily shucking the sweats down his body and off the side of the bed. He got back in his position against the pillows before Liam had even had a chance to pull down his fly.

A growl rumbled from deep in Liam's chest. He stood frozen, his eyes trained on Declan's hard length. Declan shuddered in anticipation, his cock bobbing happily under Liam's attentive gaze.

Declan wrapped a hand around his erection and gently tugged. "Are you planning to join me sometime this century?" Declan bit his lip to stop a cry of pleasure escaping.

He'd no idea where all his confidence had come from; he normally acted quiet and shy unless someone caught him in in a kitchen baking. He considered it the one domain where he could and would easily take charge.

This boldness, however, was completely new. He'd never acted with aggression towards any previous lover. Declan wondered if the fact Liam being his mate, even if they had yet to claim each other, had him acting so self-assured and knowing what he wanted.

Declan didn't realise he'd missed the grand unveiling until the mattress dipped slightly beside him when Liam crawled his way up Declan's body. Declan stopped the movement of his hand when he met Liam's gaze. Liquid silver, the effect utterly took Declan's breath away, and he reached out to his mate.

Liam turned his head slightly and pressed his lips to Declan's palm before lowering his body and kissing the leaking tip of Declan's cock. Declan moaned, loving the feel of Liam's soft mouth against his engorged flesh. Liam didn't take it any further; instead he dipped his tongue in Declan's bellybutton then made his way up Declan's chest in a line of light, barely there, touches. Each nipple received a gentle bite, then his sternum followed by his neck, his jaw, and finally his lips.

Declan melted into the sweet, gentle press of lips against his own. Liam shuddered above him as their cocks met for the first time, hard flesh against hard flesh. Declan's sounds were quickly swallowed by Liam as he deepened their kiss.

When Liam broke the contact, his lips were red and swollen, a light sheen of saliva coating them. Declan loved the fact he'd made them look that way.

"You really need to stop doing that." Declan tried to pull Liam back down.

"Stop what?" Liam asked.

"Stop stopping," Declan whined low in his throat.

"Huh?"

Liam's wicked smile had Declan thinking the man knew exactly what he did to Declan. "Every time you kiss me, you always stop right when it gets interesting. You need to stop stopping." Adamant, Declan needed that to happen.

Liam threw his head back and laughed. His body shook against Declan's. Liam's cock rubbing against his had him leaking out another drop of pre-cum.

"Liam," he whined.

He didn't want laughing. He wanted Liam fucking him through the mattress.

"You're beautiful, you know that?" Liam asked.

Declan blushed at the declaration.

"I'm so glad I finally found you."

"Technically I found you," Declan said impishly.

"Shut up and kiss me," Liam growled and mashed their mouths together once again.

Declan wouldn't argue. He sank farther into the mattress when Liam plundered his mouth. Their bodies aligned perfectly. Liam's hard, leaking shaft rubbing against his own had Declan on the verge of climax before he even realised it was possible.

Declan frantically pushed against Liam's chest, trying to get him to stop for a moment so he could breathe and try and regain some control over his errant body. Ironic, wanting Liam to stop after Declan just got through telling Liam not to, but he didn't want to come too soon. Liam took the hint and paused, looking down with a question in his eyes.

"Sorry, was about two seconds away from blowing, and I don't want to do that yet."

"Why the hell not?" Liam asked, confused.

Declan blushed. The scent of Liam's arousal

increased as the man watched him. "I don't want to come until you're buried deep inside me," he whispered with his eyes closed, too embarrassed to look at Liam when telling him what he wanted.

The deep rumbling in Liam's chest caused Declan's body to shiver with want, and he reached out to place his hand against the lightly furred skin. Liam's torso vibrated under his touch, his cock twitching with the sensations.

"Your wish is my command, honey." Liam's voice went low and sexy.

Before Declan could utter a single word, he had been flipped over, his face now buried in the pillow. He inhaled deeply, letting Liam's scent surround him. Declan's cock grew ever harder, if that was possible. Liam placed his hands on either side of Declan's hips and lifted them to the perfect height. Liam's rough, callused fingers moved and parted Declan's cheeks, exposing his clenching hole for Liam to see.

A moan tore from Declan's throat when Liam's tongue swiped across his puckered ring, then travelled down towards his balls before sliding all the way to the top of his crack. He finally zeroed back in on Declan's entrance.

Declan tilted his hips back farther when Liam's tongue speared past the first ring of muscle. Liam gently caressed Declan's hole with his thumb before he worked its way inside. Declan bit the pillow underneath him to stop from crying out at the feeling of finally being penetrated.

Declan had died and gone to heaven. Liam worked his body like a finely tuned instrument. Just when Declan thought he would come from the many sensations shooting through his body, Liam pulled back. Declan whimpered at the feeling of loss that encompassed him. His muscles twitched, his body wanting to be filled again.

Liam kissed his lower back. "My name would look perfect right here," Liam whispered, almost too quiet for Declan to hear.

Liam's thumb traced a line across Declan's back just above his crack. He suspected Liam had been talking to himself more than Declan.

"Liam," Declan said almost desperately. He needed his mate to finish what he had started.

"Coming, honey. Good things come to those who wait, you know." Liam leant over and rummaged in his bedside drawer, pulling out a half-empty bottle of lube.

Thoughts of why the bottle would be half-empty and of men, other than himself, in his mate's bed had Declan's wolf coming to the surface. His canines lengthened, his eyes shifted, and a loud growl escaped his chest, no matter how hard he tried to hold the damn thing back.

Liam looked at him with the biggest grin Declan had ever seen on anyone. "God, you're hot when you're jealous, all part shifted. Your eyes are really something."

"I'm not jealous." Even Declan didn't believe the words when they came out of his mouth.

"Really?" Liam asked with a raised eyebrow as he shook the tube of lube.

Declan snarled, which only caused Liam's smile to widen. "See, hot as fuck. I can't wait to feel those teeth sink into my flesh."

"If you don't get a move on, you will be feeling them a lot sooner than you think."

Liam didn't reply. Instead he smacked Declan's ass hard twice, once on either cheek. Declan sucked in a breath, intense pleasure shooting through his body at the contact. The spanking definitely deserved further exploration in the future.

The snick of the lube opening had Declan wiggling his ass; he didn't care if it made him look wanton. He wanted to feel his mate deep inside of him. Now, dammit!

* * * *

Liam took a steadying breath and coated his fingers with slick. He was about two seconds away from blowing like a teenager. Having his mate in bed, wiggling his ass, begging to be fucked had to be Liam's greatest fantasy come to life.

He quickly coated his cock, careful not to linger too

long in case he lost control at the image Declan made, then settled between his spread legs.

Liam gently circled Declan's tight pucker before pushing two fingers deep inside his mate. A gasp followed by a low groan of pleasure told Liam all he needed to know about Declan's state of readiness. Liam pumped his fingers in and out of Declan's body. The tight ring of muscle did everything in its power to keep Liam within its hold. Liam added a third finger and continued to stretch Declan.

"Liam, would you get a move on and fuck me already?" Declan cried as he thrust his hips back once again to meet Liam's fingers.

"With pleasure, honey."

"Thank God." Liam laughed at the relief in Declan's voice.

Liam removed his fingers, gripped the base of his erection, and scooted forward.

"Ready?" The angry snarl he got in return said enough. He plunged forward, burying his cock completely in Declan's quivering heat. "Shit," he muttered, gripping Declan's hips, holding him still.

Liam dragged air into his lungs, trying not to come too quickly. The clenching walls surrounding his bare dick felt like nothing he had ever experienced before. Every clench and contraction of Declan's ass held him tight within its depths.

"Move, Goddamn you!" his feisty mate growled.

Liam slowly pulled out and spanked Declan hard on his left cheek before plunging in again. A loud groan of approval and the heavy scent of lust in the air showed Declan's enjoyment of their mating.

Liam started thrusting into his mate like a man possessed. His wolf rose to the surface, his eyes changed, his teeth elongated, and his claws grew. The long curve of his nails dug into Declan's skin, and the tangy scent of coppery blood hit Liam like a freight train.

He pulled Declan up to a kneeling position, never losing rhythm, and Liam carefully wrapped his fist around Declan's straining shaft, giving it a hard tug.

He leant forward, using his other hand to haul Declan's head back against his left shoulder. Liam rasped his tongue across his mate's sweaty skin, letting him know what would happen next.

"Come for me," he whispered a moment before he bit down, joining them together as mates for the rest of their lives.

Declan screamed. The cock in his hand grew impossibly hard before it exploded, shooting white strings of cum over the bed beneath them.

Liam drew Declan's blood into his mouth, cementing their bond, and Declan's ass clamped down around the base of Liam's cock. Liam released Declan's neck, crying out in completion when his orgasm filled his mate to bursting. Liam panted. The pleasure he'd just experienced increased when the mating knot extended from his cock and latched onto Declan's prostate.

Declan shuddered when another orgasm ignited his body before he collapsed back against Liam, his eyes rolling up. Liam quickly caught Declan before he could fall off the bed.

Still joined together, Liam lowered them gently to the side of the wet patch and drew his mate close. Liam had never felt anything so intense in his life, little shocks still travelling through his body, and his cock, still buried deep within Declan, throbbed in pleasure.

Liam had no idea how he would survive if their coming together would be like this every time. He kissed Declan on the back of the head and settled down to wait for their bodies to unlock, happy in the knowledge he held his mate in his arms.

<u>Chapter Seven</u>

Nervousness radiated through Declan as Liam drove them towards his Alpha's house. Not only would he meet the Pennaeth Alpha of all of Australia's many packs, but the man also happened to be one of Liam's closest friends. He really didn't want to do anything that would embarrass his mate or cause of any friction between them. He didn't even want to think about the card game afterward with even more strangers. Declan had no idea how to play poker.

His mum had always taught him that when he went to someone's house never to show up empty-handed. As a pastry chef, Declan often baked goods to take when he visited someone, as he had found himself doing earlier in the afternoon.

He'd been surprised at how well-stocked Liam's fridge and pantry had been for a bachelor. After reviewing his available ingredients, Declan settled on chocolate éclairs and a rich caramel slice. It helped to pass the day and get his mind off witnessing a murder. He'd spoken with his brother briefly at lunchtime, and Tommy and his friends had been able to retrieve Declan's car with no worries. Relief filled Declan when Tommy told him that he hadn't seen or spoken with Alpha Wallis.

Two less problems to deal with, especially when, after he and Liam had recovered from their vigorous mating, Declan realized he had no clothes. He'd arrived on Liam's doorstep naked. He'd worn the sweat pants Liam had given him all day, but he refused to show up at the Pennaeth Alpha's house and meet Liam's friends in nothing but a pair of hand-me-downs from his mate.

Liam kissed him soundly, told Declan to finish what he'd interrupted when he'd arrived home, and he would go get him some clothes.

Declan managed to cut and plate the caramel slice that had firmed to perfection in the fridge and finished filling all the éclair shells, covering them all with chocolate. He decided after seeing Liam's different varieties to cover some with dark, some with milk, and some with white. Everybody had their own favourites, and he'd hit all the bases by using some of each.

Declan couldn't even begin to express his gratitude that werewolves didn't share a canine's inability to metabolize and digest chocolate. Declan didn't know how he'd cope if he was allergic to the sweet.

He had just finished cleaning the last dish when Liam returned carrying several bags. Pleased with the selection of clothes Liam had gotten for him, Declan thanked this mate. Nothing was fancy or over the top, just clothes Declan knew he would be comfortable wearing. He also noticed the distinct lack of underwear, and when he commented, Liam simply shrugged and told him they were out. Yeah right, like he believed that. Declan wouldn't argue, though. If his mate liked the idea of him going commando, Declan had no problem with it.

Dressed in jeans, runners, a shirt, and a light jacket, Declan sat in the passenger seat of Liam's car as they headed to their destination. His foot started tapping on the floorboards, and he held onto his pastries and watched the town they drove through. He jumped when Liam's hand settled on his leg.

"Relax, Declan. Everything will be fine."

Declan tried to relax his jittery leg. He took deep breaths, but it didn't really help the situation when his lungs filled up with the scent of his mate. Arousal growing, his body started to respond to the touch of Liam's hand on his leg, especially when Liam started inching his fingers higher up Declan's thigh.

"Liam."

"What?" his mate asked all innocent-like.

"You know what," he replied.

Liam didn't pay any attention, and his hand continued to inch higher. "Sorry, I'm afraid I have no idea what you're talking about." The mischievous glint in Liam's eyes told another story, though.

"There is no way in hell I am going to meet your Alpha and friends sporting a hard-on that will be extra noticeable because you refused to buy me any underwear."

"I did no such thing." Liam obviously was trying his best to sound shocked at the accusation, but the smile tugging at his lips really didn't help his cause. "I told you the store ran out."

"Right." He still didn't believe that.

Liam laughed and Declan smiled back. It felt good to banter light-heartedly with his mate. Declan had never had someone he could do that with before.

"Come on, babe. Time to go." Liam turned off the car and opened the door.

"What? We're there already?" he asked, not sure if he was ready.

"Yep." Liam exited the car and walked around the front and opened Declan's door. "Come on, babe, everything is going to be fine. I'll introduce you to Ben then we can have a little talk about what brought you to my door, naked."

Liam waggled his brows, and Declan couldn't help but laugh. Declan leant into the hand caressing his cheek before turning and placing a quick kiss against Liam's palm.

"Then we'll gather with the guys and play some cards. Everyone will love you, I guarantee it. They'll all be so happy that I found my mate, it will give them hope that they, too, will one day find theirs."

Declan didn't know if he completely believed what Liam said, but he'd only find out one way. Taking a deep breath, he unclipped his seatbelt. Holding onto the desserts like they were a lifeline, Declan got out of the car.

Liam gave him a quick kiss before breaking away

and placing his hand on the small of Declan's back when they made their way up the walk to the Alpha's front door. Declan chewed on his bottom lip the entire way. When they reached the entrance, Declan expected them to stop and wait. Instead Liam knocked on the door loudly before pushing it open and walking inside, encouraging Declan along with the hand still on his lower back.

"Ben," Liam yelled out.

What the hell? Liam could just barge into the Alpha's house without being admitted first? Declan had never seen such a thing. If anyone had tried that with Alpha Wallis's house, they would have found themselves in a fight, if not worse.

"Come on back, Liam. I'm in the office." A deep booming voice carried to them from down a hall.

Declan shivered at the sheer power contained in that voice.

Declan looked at his mate, still not sure about meeting Ben, but Liam continued to smile as he led him through the house. They reached an open door and Liam rapped lightly on the wooden surface before walking into the office. Declan tried to hang back, but Liam wouldn't let him.

The large man sitting behind his desk looked up from what he had been doing on his computer. If Declan thought his mate tall, the man sitting behind the desk must be close on giant sized. Even while seated, Declan could tell he would stand at least six and a half feet, if not a little taller. He had broad shoulders, dark brown, almost black hair, a five o'clock shadow that looked more permanent than not, and the most piercing blue eyes Declan had ever seen.

"Ben, I have the great satisfaction of introducing you to my mate, Declan Morgan. Declan, this is the Pennaeth Alpha, Benjamin Taylor."

"Well congratulations, Liam," Alpha Taylor said as a broad smile appeared. "I know how long you've looked for your mate." Ben stood, showing no surprise about his friend suddenly appearing with a mate, and walked around the desk.

Declan quickly realised he'd correctly guessed the man's height. Yep, must have giant blood somewhere in his ancestry. Ben stepped up, his hand out. Declan looked down at his, both still holding onto the sweets they had brought.

Liam, seeing his dilemma, took the containers, and Declan reached out to shake the Alpha's outstretched hand. The sheer power pouring from the man in front of him had Declan's wolf wanting to roll over and expose his belly. To satisfy his urges, Declan tilted his head to the side, exposing his neck. Alpha Taylor acknowledged him with a gentle touch.

Liam spoke. "Thank you, Ben. I can't tell you how happy I am to have finally found Declan." His mate wore a huge smile.

It looked good on him. His entire face seemed to light up.

"Declan, welcome. I hope you will consider making the Atherton pack your home," Ben said.

"Yes, Alpha. I would be honoured." Declan couldn't believe the easy acceptance the Alpha offered. Humbled to belong to Benjamin Taylor's pack, Declan truly hoped he could one day count the man as a friend.

"Now, why don't you tell me how you two met? Come take a seat and we can talk." Ben gestured to a comfortable-looking couch-and-chair combo off in one corner of the large office.

"If you'll excuse me for a moment, Ben, I'll go and put these in the fridge for later." Liam exited the room before Declan could even call him back. He looked at Ben and hastily moved in the direction of the couch and took a seat.

"Relax, mate. Everything is going to be fine." Declan jumped nearly a foot off the couch when he heard Liam's voice inside his head.

A chuckle opposite him took his attention away from his mate for a moment, and he saw amusement on the Alpha's face.

"I take it that's the first time you've used the mate link?"

"Umm. Yeah. To tell you the truth, I had completely forgotten all about it." Declan could feel the blush creeping up his cheeks. Thankfully Liam walked back into the office and headed over to take a seat next to him on the couch.

"What did you need to put in the fridge?" Alpha Taylor asked in obvious curiosity.

"Declan is a pastry chef."

"Is that so?" the Alpha asked.

"Yes, sir."

"Please, call me Ben. I don't stand on formality in my own home."

"Thank you, Ben." Declan didn't think he had met another Alpha quite like Ben Taylor. "My mother always taught me never to show up at someone's house empty-handed, so I made a couple of desserts."

"I can't wait to taste them."

Declan blushed again.

"Now back to my original question. How did the two of you meet?" Ben asked.

"Would you believe he showed up on my doorstep last night naked?" Liam said casually.

"No, I wouldn't." Ben laughed.

Heat rose once again to Declan's cheeks.

"Seriously?" Ben asked, looking a little astounded.

"Yeah. I was in the middle of cooking dinner and I turned around and there he stood on my back porch, naked as the day he came into the world and freezing his very sexy ass off," Liam answered.

Ben seemed to think over what Liam had just said before he turned in Declan's direction and asked the one question he had been dreading.

"What brought you to Atherton in your shifted form, Declan?"

Declan took a deep breath and exhaled loudly. He hadn't done anything wrong, but the sound of the gun being discharged still haunted him. He had done everything possible today to keep himself busy so he didn't have time to stop and think about what he'd witnessed.

Liam reached over and took his hand, squeezing it gently. *"Please, honey, we can't help if you don't tell us what's happened."*

Declan nodded. Liam spoke the truth. Ben needed to be told about what had happened, but it didn't stop him from being scared.

Declan looked down at this hands, marvelling at the difference between his and his mate's. His hands were white, almost porcelain as he spent so much of his day indoors, whereas Liam's were a nice rich olive colour, the black of his tattoo standing out even against his darker skin tone. It was a distraction from having to talk about what came next, Declan knew. He also knew he couldn't avoid it no matter how much he might want to.

"I witnessed my Alpha kill a pack member," he finally answered, his voice barely more than a whisper.

Ben took a moment before he spoke. "There's nothing new in that. Challenges for the Alpha position sometimes end in death. As much as I hate to admit that, it's a way of life for wolves."

Declan completely got the survival of the fittest concept. His old pack Alpha had gotten the position in a fight to the death. If he'd witnessed the ritual, there wouldn't be a problem. But that wasn't the case.

"It wasn't a challenge for Alpha." Declan paused for a moment before ploughing on. "Kegan Wallis, Alpha of the Cairns pack, murdered my packmate, Nigel Cummings, in cold blood over drugs."

Liam whistled beside him. Declan finally raised his eyes from their joined hands and looked first at his mate, then towards Ben. Ben sat back in his chair and scrubbed his hands down his face. The man looked tired all of a sudden.

"I'm sorry," he whispered.

Ben looked at him. "You have absolutely nothing to be sorry for. I would like to hear the complete story, though, please."

Declan nodded.

Not sure where to start, Declan figured right at the beginning would probably be better than skipping a whole lot and not giving the Alpha all the information.

Declan told how he and his brother had come to live in Cairns. He also mentioned not having many friends within the pack and how few meetings he actually attended.

"The meetings I did attend, I didn't like very much, and Alpha Kegan Wallis, in my opinion, is an asshole and a sleaze. Three-quarters of the pack are scared of him, but the others seem to love him and even cheer him on. Unfortunately no member of their pack is anywhere near strong enough to challenge him for the job.

"Saturday night I was feeling a little sorry for myself after an exhausting day at work. As usual, I found myself alone with nothing to do and nowhere to go, so I decided to go for a run. It had been a while since I had been able to shift and let my wolf roam free, so I headed out to our pack lands and changed."

Declan looked around to make sure he hadn't lost his listeners so far. They nodded at him to continue, so he settled back, leaning against Liam's side and drawing strength from his mate. Liam wrapped his arm around his shoulders and pulled him in tight.

"I was in the middle of a nice juicy rabbit when I heard angry voices coming through the trees. I reluctantly abandoned my late dinner and went to investigate." Declan paused again to gather himself.

No please, it wasn't me, you have to believe m— Nigel's voice echoed through Declan's head right before being cut off permanently.

Declan flinched when the sound of the gun reverberated in his mind over and over. Before he knew what had happened, Declan found himself in his mate's lap. It should have been awkward given his size, but instead he fit perfectly. Liam's arms were wrapped around him, the man making gentle shushing noises in his ear as Declan shook.

Declan held onto his mate as tightly as he could, burying his face in Liam's neck, not wanting to lose the connection they had.

"Shh, honey, everything is okay. Calm down. Breathe for me."

Declan nodded but he didn't let go of Liam.

"Declan. Breathe!" Liam's sharp tone cut through his mind.

Declan exhaled in a rush and sucked air back into his aching lungs. He'd had no idea he'd been holding his breath.

When his body finally calmed down, Declan pulled back slightly and looked in to the beautiful silver eyes of his man. "I'm sorry."

"You have nothing to be sorry about, honey. Everyone deals with things differently and I think things just caught up with you."

Declan nodded. He had been wondering why he had been so calm about everything. Declan laid his head back down against Liam's chest and settled in, closing his eyes while Liam rubbed soothing circles along his back.

Declan told them in a quiet, shaky voice about what he had witnessed—the beating, the argument about the drugs, and finally the murder of his packmate. "Oh God. There was so much blood. Nigel's head went back with the force of the bullet, and then he collapsed between the two Betas who just dropped his body like he was nothing but a piece of garbage."

Liam's arms tightened, pulling Declan even closer. Gentle kisses were placed on the top of his head.

"Jesus H Christ," Ben exploded behind them.

Declan opened his eyes. The Alpha got up and started pacing his office.

"I didn't want to hang around, so I tried to back away and leave, but I stepped on a branch and it snapped under my paw, drawing their attention directly to me. I wasn't going to stay and find out what they would do to me, so I bolted. They gave chase.

"If it wasn't for my speed, I think I'd probably be dead now. Even with my speed, I ran for hours on end." Nothing like a good dose of fear to push him to his limits. "It took a while until the sounds of chase died away, but I didn't know what else to do. I couldn't just turn around and go home like nothing had happened, so I kept going in the direction I had been chased and eventually ended up here." Even with what had led him here, Declan couldn't be upset with the outcome so far. "Once I spotted the town, I kept mainly to the outskirts until I smelt the most alluring scent. I followed it, and it led me to you," Declan finished as he looked at his mate.

"Thank God for that," Liam said, and he brought his hands up to cup Declan's cheeks.

Liam bent down slightly and took Declan's mouth in the sweetest, gentlest kiss.

When Liam finally broke the embrace, he leaned back and looked Declan in the eyes. "I hate what you went through to get here. If I could take it away, I would do it in a heartbeat. I can't be sorry, though, that you found me. I've been looking for a very long time for you, and I'm not going to give you up for anything. Not even a deranged, drug-dealing Alpha, you hear me?"

Declan nodded and his eyes filled with tears. He buried his head once again in Liam's chest and listened to Ben pace behind him, swearing repeatedly.

Speaking about the murder brought all his concerns once again to the surface, highlighting just how vulnerable his brother could be if the Alpha decided to go after him.

Ben's constant back and forth didn't do anything to help Declan's wild thoughts. "I need to get Tommy. I don't know how safe he is, and I have no idea if Alpha Wallis will try and use him to get to me or not. But I need my brother. He's the only family I have left."

<u>Chapter Eight</u>

Liam wanted to shout that Declan had more than his brother now. He had Liam and Liam's entire family. He knew, however, now wouldn't be a good time; instead he held his mate tight and kissed the top of his head. Liam didn't think he'd ever been so angry in his life at what Declan had been through. He couldn't begin to imagine how scared Declan must have been to be chased for so long through unfamiliar territory after witnessing what he had.

Liam couldn't get his head around how strong his feelings towards his mate were already. They'd only known each other for twenty-four hours. It felt like a lifetime.

Before Liam, or anyone else, could say anything, the sound of knocking came from the direction of the front door, followed by the loud voices of Liam and Ben's friends.

"Yo, assholes, hope you're ready to have your asses handed to you," Corey yelled out.

"As if, you couldn't win if your life depended on it," Sam snickered behind him.

"Like you could," Brad started in.

"Everyone knows it's me who goes home with the pot every week." Kieran's soft voice carried into the room with them.

Liam smiled. They were all full of shit, but they were

the best friends a guy could have. He looked at Ben for a moment and saw the man fighting a smile of his own.

"There's nothing we can do tonight, Declan. Trust me to handle this and make your brother safe. First thing tomorrow we'll start sorting this mess out," Ben said gently.

Declan nodded against Liam's chest.

"Take a couple of minutes. I'll get the guys settled. Come out when you're ready." Ben left the office, closing the door behind him. It didn't stop the sound of his voice from being heard clearly through the wood. "All right, you bunch of idiots, settle down. Are we gonna play poker or stand around gasbagging like a bunch of old ladies in the CWA?"

Declan snickered.

"Where's Liam?" Brad asked.

"He'll be out in a minute."

Thankfully Ben didn't tell them about Declan; Liam really wanted to see their faces when he introduced his mate.

"You okay, honey?" Liam asked softly.

"Not sure. Your friends seem, umm… nice?"

Liam laughed. "Is that a question or a statement?" he asked, still chuckling.

"Ah, both?" Declan looked so uncertain.

Liam smiled and kissed his mate. Declan was incredible, and Liam really started to look forward to the life they would have together.

"The guys are great, you'll love them. Corey, Kieran, and I grew up together. Ben, Brad, and Sam are all just ring-ins." Declan laughed, just as Liam had hoped.

"I would love to see you tell the Alpha to his face that he's just a ring-in."

"So not happening. I might love the guy like a brother, but I'm not completely stupid. The only reason Corey gets away with it is because we can't stop him. The man has no brain-to-mouth filter. He says exactly what he thinks.

"The only time he shows a modicum of decorum is when other pack members are in attendance, and even then it's touch-and-go. Unless he's on official Beta business, then he becomes the most focused individual you'll ever meet. Bradley, on the other hand, is a more relaxed Beta, like me."

Liam smoothed his hands down his mate's body, glad the trembling had completely stopped. "Come on, beautiful, I want to introduce you to my friends."

Declan nodded slowly before crawling off Liam's lap to stand. As much as Liam wanted to go see his friends, he wished Declan didn't have to get up to do it. The man felt wonderful in his arms, and Liam wanted him back there as soon as possible.

Liam cupped Declan's cheek before leaning in and kissing him senseless. Declan moaned when Liam's tongue invaded his mouth. Liam pulled Declan against his body, and Declan's cock responded to his touch.

Liam's dick came to life as if in answer. Reluctantly, he broke the wonderful embrace. The glazed look in Declan's eyes when he blinked rapidly, trying to clear his vision, made Liam smile with happiness.

"Just a little something to think about until I can get you home and naked again," Liam whispered in Declan's ear before taking the lobe between his teeth and biting down gently.

Declan moaned loudly and thrust his groin into Liam's. "Can't we go now?" he panted.

"Nope, you're not getting out of this, no matter how much I want to strip you naked and lick you from top to bottom," Liam rasped, sliding his hand down between their bodies and cupping Declan's hard cock through his jeans.

"Jesus. Can you stop please?" Declan whimpered but continued to push into Liam's hand. "It's bad enough I'm about to meet your friends with a raging hard-on, but if you don't stop talking like that, I'll be meeting them with a wet patch as well."

Liam laughed. He loved the effect he had on his mate. Stepping back, Liam grabbed Declan's hand and headed for the door to the office before Declan's brain could catch up to what they were doing.

Dragging his mate behind him, Liam walked through Ben's house until they came to the dining room where his friends were all settled around the table, poker chips separated into six equal piles. Beers sat in front of each player with one currently placed by his customary seat as well. There were small bowls of snacks on the table at each end. Nothing large, just something to nibble on while they played. They would order pizza or Chinese later, depending on what everyone felt like. Kieran was shuffling the deck of playing cards.

All conversation stopped when Liam entered the room still holding Declan's hand. Nervousness rolled off Declan in waves. He really wished he could say or do something to calm his mate, but time would tell. These were a great bunch of guys. Loud and rowdy at times, but great nonetheless.

Liam pulled Declan against his side when everyone turned to look at the pair. "Declan, meet the guys. You know Ben. Going round the table, on Ben's right is Kieran, then Brad, Sam, and Corey." Everyone nodded when Liam said their names.

Keeping his tone low-key, Liam said, "Guys, this is Declan Morgan. My mate." Liam didn't have to wait long for the expected reaction.

"Your what?" Sam asked.

"Since when? Man, I only saw you yesterday morning. You didn't mention anything about a mate," Brad said.

"Wow, he's hot," Corey said and whistled low and appreciatively.

Liam narrowed his eyes and growled, baring his teeth. Corey just laughed. Liam noticed Ben sitting to the side smiling along as well.

"Congratulation, Liam," Kieran said quietly after the others had finished.

Kieran got up from his seat and came round the table, hand out ready to shake. "It's a pleasure to meet you, Declan. You couldn't have a better mate than Liam here. I hope you two will be very happy together."

Declan's cheeks were bright red when he shook hands with Kieran before his friend headed back to his seat at the table.

Liam had a sudden thought. "Honey, do you know how to play poker?"

Declan's cheeks went even redder as he shook his head.

"That's okay, you can sit with me, and I'll teach you everything you need to know to win the game," Liam said as they headed to the two empty chairs at the head of the table.

"If he wants to win, then he should be sitting with me," Brad commented.

"Bullshit," Corey fake-coughed.

"All right, all right, are we gonna play or not, gentleman?" Ben asked.

"Just waiting on the cards," Sam piped up.

"Hold your damn horses. God, don't get your knickers in a twist." Kieran huffed and started dealing the cards for Texas hold 'em poker.

They settled down for a couple of rounds, Liam

doing his best to explain the game in a way Declan could understand. He didn't know if it helped or not that every time he explained something, one of the guys would add their own piece of advice into the mix.

A half hour later they put in a call for pizza delivery and went back to playing. Corey broke first and asked questions about where Declan had come from just as Liam expected.

"So, Declan, how did the two of you meet?"

Declan waited for Corey to take a long swallow from his beer before he answered. "I turned up on his doorstep —naked—last night."

Liam burst out laughing when Corey choked and sprayed beer everywhere. Poor Ben, sitting opposite Corey at the table, got drenched in beer and spit as Corey continued to splutter, trying to get his breath back. The others all cracked up at seeing Corey completely lost for words and Ben covered in beer.

Ben growled, but Corey could only hold up a hand in apology, still unable to talk. Ben got up, and before stalking from the room, pointed to the mess on the table.

He directed his gaze towards Corey. "Clean this shit up, man."

Liam assumed he'd go wipe himself down and change his shirt.

"Man, that was fucking priceless," Brad said between gasping breaths.

Kieran chuckled quietly and got up, heading to the

kitchen to grab something to wipe the table down with.

Liam glanced at his mate, who sat with a satisfied look on his face. Liam pulled him to his side and wrapped his arm around Declan's shoulder. *"Beautiful timing, honey."*

"Thanks."

Ben entered the room a couple of minutes later and looked at Corey, raising a brow in question. "You all better now?" he asked, sarcasm dripping from his voice.

"Yeah, man. Sorry 'bout that."

Ben huffed, crossing his arms over his chest when he settled back in his chair.

"What the hell is taking you so long, Kieran?" Sam called out.

A muffled sound came from the direction of the kitchen and a moment later Kieran finally came back into the room, damp cloth and paper towels in hand. His face however, not quite as clean as it had been when he left.

"What the hell? It looks like you blew someone back there. Jesus, is there a sale on naked men running around town or something that I don't know about?" Corey asked.

Kieran looked guilty as hell; his tongue flicked out and cleaned the white substance from the side of his mouth. "It's cream, you idiot."

"Cream?" Poor Corey just sounded confused now.

"Yeah, I found a stash of desserts in Ben's fridge

when I went looking for another beer." Kieran closed his eyes and moaned. "The caramel slice tasted unlike any I've ever had before, so good. And the éclairs. Don't even get me started. I think I might skip dinner altogether and go straight to the desserts."

"Since when do you stock desserts for poker night?" Brad asked Ben.

"Since Declan is a pastry chef and brought them. Though I haven't yet had a chance to taste them myself. Unlike some, I have restraint."

All eyes turned once again to Declan and Liam.

Declan sat up straight and shrugged. Liam liked the fact his mate wouldn't be embarrassed about doing something he enjoyed. Liam felt a tiny bit jealous of Kieran. He had yet to try Declan's creations either.

"Man, you need to stick around and cook. They were sinfully delicious," Kieran said as he headed for the beer-sprayed section of the table.

"Thanks, man. Glad you enjoyed," Declan replied.

"Now this I have to try," Sam said as he pushed back his chair.

"Sit," Ben barked. "You can wait like the rest of us. Don't worry, they're not going anywhere."

Kieran quickly cleaned the table, and everyone settled back down again to play cards. The doorbell rang twenty minutes later, announcing the arrival of the pizza. Everyone threw a ten on the pile, and Liam got up with Brad to take delivery. Along with four large pizzas they had three garlic breads and two side serves of ribs.

Delivery paid for, they took the food back to the guys.

After setting the pizzas down, Liam headed to the kitchen, calling out on his way, "Who wants another beer?"

Affirmative yells came at him left, right, and centre. Declan followed him when it became apparent he would be getting everyone another drink. Liam was good, but even he couldn't carry seven beers by himself.

"Enjoying yourself?" he asked Declan when they were in the kitchen, pulling the drinks from the fridge.

"Yeah, you were right. They're a great bunch of guys."

"Told you." Liam grabbed the last two beers and closed the fridge before he could be tempted to steal one of the éclairs.

He turned around and quickly kissed Declan, who stood directly behind him. "Come on, we better get back out there before all the food disappears."

They headed back, handed out the beers to everyone, and settled down to eat some pizza and garlic bread. They usually paused the game when it came time to eat dinner. Corey had just finished his third slice and reached for a fourth when he threw a sideways glance in Declan's direction.

"So, he really rocked up on your doorstep naked?" he asked.

"Yep, I was cooking dinner, turned around and there he stood, in all his naked glory, on my back porch."

"Ah man, some people have all the luck," Brad complained.

"Why can't naked men show up on my doorstop?" Sam asked.

Liam laughed and kissed Declan on the side of his head before taking another bite of pizza.

They picked up the game again after finishing the food and the pile of chips in front of Liam grew to three times the size of any of the other guys. "You must be my lucky charm," Liam whispered in Declan's ear before he pecked him on the cheek and threw in three chips, raising the pot.

Kieran folded his hand and got up from the table, heading to the kitchen. Ben looked down at his cards one more time before seeing his bet. They were the last two in this pot.

"All right, old man, what have you got?" Liam asked.

"That's enough with the 'old man' comments, thank you very much," Ben mock growled

Liam laughed.

Ben set his cards down on the table. "Full house, aces over threes."

Liam kept his expression neutral. "Two pair," he said.

Ben whooped and leant in to sweep the chips to his

seat.

Liam placed his hand on Ben's arm. "Not so fast, old man." He smirked before turning his cards over.

Ben looked down at the pair of threes Liam had had in his hand before glancing at the pair of threes in the centre of the table. "Asshole."

"Who's an asshole?" Kieran asked as he walked back into the room carrying Declan's desserts. "Sorry, couldn't wait any longer."

"Liam," Ben huffed.

"Well, we all knew that, though Declan might not yet, but give him enough time, and I'm sure he'll agree," Corey added his two cents.

Liam swept the chips, and Kieran made use of the empty space by placing down a tray filled with éclairs and another one with caramel slices.

Everyone reached in at exactly the same time, giving Liam the impression of starving animals that hadn't eaten in weeks. Liam grabbed for a caramel slice as sounds of appreciation filled the room.

"Oh God, this is good," Corey moaned in pleasure.

"What the hell did you put in this cream?" Brad asked.

"That caramel is the best I've ever tasted," Ben commented.

Liam gazed at Declan. Happiness and pure pleasure radiated from him. Liam bit into a corner of his caramel slice, and his groans of pleasure soon added to those of his friends.

The chocolate biscuit base, the thick layer of rich gooey caramel, and the thin covering of chocolate all combined to make one of the best things Liam had ever had in his mouth, not including his mate, of course.

"Jesus, you have got to try this caramel slice," he mumbled around another mouthful.

"Same goes for the éclairs," Kieran said and again reached into the centre of the table.

Once Liam had finished his piece of heaven, he reached in for Declan's other creation. The desserts had gone quickly as there were only a couple left of each. Not wanting to miss out, Liam grabbed two éclairs and another slice and put them reverently on the table in front of him.

Declan laughed. "You do realise if you miss out, I can always make you some more?"

"Not the point." He grunted and picked up an éclair, biting it in half. Holy mother, they were just as good as the slice.

"Marry me?"

Liam shook his head. The question hadn't come from his mouth. He looked out over the table and saw Brad staring at his mate with a look Liam had no idea how to describe.

Liam slammed his hands on the table as he quickly stood and snarled. "Mine!" Fury like never before rolled through his body: someone had attempted to take his mate away from him.

"Whoa, dude, calm down," Corey hastily said.

"Liam," Ben said calmly from his seat.

Liam didn't care, though. None of his friends had mates. None of them understood the emotions raging through his body at that point in time. Just the thought of someone trying to take Declan from him caused him to lose his shit, even if that man happened to be a good friend of his.

"Liam." Declan's soft voice floated through his mind, calming him down to more a rumbling growl instead of outright snarling.

Declan caressed his arm to calm him further. *"Babe, you know it was a joke. Calm down. I'm yours. You don't need to worry about that."*

Brad stood behind both Corey and Sam, looking a little pale. Liam bared his teeth one last time and turned, pulling Declan into his arms before anyone could so much as blink.

He slammed his mouth down onto his mate's and demanded entrance. The need to prove Declan still belonged to him had him shaking so badly he thought he would fall apart. Declan opened immediately, their tongues tangling as Liam plundered Declan's willing mouth. Declan's arms wrapped around his neck, and Liam pulled him in tight. Their hard cocks rubbed against each other through the thick fabric of their jeans.

Declan whimpered. Liam knew just how he felt. He

wanted his mate under him right now. Breaking the kiss reluctantly, Liam sucked in some much-needed oxygen. Declan tried to chase his lips and reinitiate the kiss.

"Let's go home, mate. I want to feel you under me," Liam said.

The needy little whine from Declan nearly did Liam in.

"I think you should apologise to Brad. He didn't mean anything by his comment."

Liam didn't like it, but Declan spoke the truth. He had overreacted.

Liam looked at Brad. "Sorry, man. Instinct. It's still brand new. Can't control my reactions at the moment."

"No worries. I should have thought before I spoke. I really just wanted to tell Declan he's an amazing pastry chef."

"Thank you," Declan said.

"All right, gentlemen, we're out of here. You can split my chips. I have something more important requiring my attention at the moment." Liam really didn't care what they did with his winnings—Declan had all his focus at the minute.

"I'll walk you out," Ben said and stood up from the table.

After walking to the door, Ben put a hand on Declan's shoulder. "I'll need a couple of days to locate a new Alpha and Betas to take over. I'll let you know when we can head on down." Ben sighed heavily.

"Unfortunately I can't leave an entire pack with no one in charge. Declan, keep in contact with your brother. You let me know the minute he tells you something's wrong."

"Will do. Thank you, Ben."

Liam steered Declan out the front door, his hands never once still on his mate's body as they walked to the car.

Chapter Nine

Declan wanted to fly apart in a million different directions as they stood beside the car. First a kiss and now Mr Grabby. Liam was driving him nuts. One second he would be feeling Declan's ass before he moved his hands round and cupped his cock, and then he would trail them up his torso and pinch his nipples. His dick ached from being so hard and confined behind his restrictive jeans. Declan thought he might be in danger of shooting in his pants right in the middle of the Alpha's front yard.

He leant back against Liam's hard, muscled chest and decided to let his mate's hands roam free. Liam gave one final squeeze to Declan's aching length before he stepped back and unlocked the car.

"Get in." Liam's voice went low, guttural and filled with heat.

Shivers ran down Declan's spine, causing tingling in his balls, and his cock throbbed painfully in his now-too-tight pants.

Liam cleared his throat, the sound farther away than it should have been, and Declan opened his eyes. When had he closed them? Liam stood by the other side of the car, door already open, waiting for Declan to get in.

"You coming?" Liam asked, looking rather smug.

Declan flipped him off and opened his car door. Liam laughed and got in the car. Declan settled back, put his seatbelt on, and waited for Liam to take off.

Once they were on the road, Declan decided to have a little fun. He reached down and pulled the lever, lowering the back of his seat so he sat more horizontal then vertical. He never would have had the confidence to do what he planned if not for Liam's constant support. The fact that meeting all Liam's friends hadn't been a disaster and they all seemed to like Declan helped a great deal as well.

"What are you doing?" Liam asked, heat lacing his words.

Declan ignored him and flicked the button open on his jeans. After grabbing the tab to his zipper, he lowered it slowly. Almost painfully slowly. Declan heard the click of every set of teeth on the zipper being undone.

Declan parted the edges of his jeans and his cock happily sprang free, his slit already wet from pre-cum, his shaft a dusty pink colour. He reached down and wrapped his fist around the base of his cock before slowly starting to jack himself. His head rolled back against the headrest, eyes closed, and his back bowed with the pleasure currently swamping his body.

Liam hissed beside him and the car slowed down, but he was too caught up in his own pleasure to notice more than that. Declan wanted more room to move, so he kicked his sneakers off and pushed his jeans down his legs as far as they would go, working one leg free.

No longer constrained by the denim, Declan put one

foot up against the dash and cupped his balls with his other hand and continued to pleasure himself.

"Fuck, you look so hot like that." Liam's raspy voice sent shivers through Declan's body.

Declan moaned as Liam undid his seatbelt and reached, his fingers joining in the pleasure. Declan knew his body was still well stretched from their previous encounter. Liam circled his hole once before plunging two fingers deep inside Declan's body. Declan cried out as he tightened his hand around his cock and increased its speed.

He could feel his release waiting at the edge, just needing one more thing to topple him over.

Liam leant over and plunged a third finger inside him at the same time he bit down on Declan's nipple through his shirt. Declan screamed when the orgasm ripped through him. Strings of pearly white cum splattered against his shirt as Liam continued his assault on Declan's body.

When the last shudder of his release left Declan, Liam withdrew his fingers, ripped open his jeans, and pushed his seat back as far as it would go.

"Get your sexy ass over here now," Liam growled, spitting on his hand and coating his cock. "Sorry, babe, but this is going to be hard and fast."

Declan nodded and scrambled over the centre console, settling in Liam's lap facing him. The look in Liam's eyes was one Declan didn't think he'd ever get tired of seeing. Liam had his fist gripped tightly around his dick, guiding it to Declan's entrance.

Declan hissed at the intense burn when Liam's head breached the first ring of muscles, then slammed home. Declan inhaled sharply, and Liam stilled beneath him.

"Sorry."

"It's fine. Just need a moment." Declan nodded and worked his ass up before sliding back down slowly.

Liam gripped his hips, holding them in place, and began thrusting in and out of Declan's ass like his life depended on it. Declan's shaft came back to life and filled with renewed vigour when, time after time, Liam pegged his sweet spot.

Declan fisted his hands in Liam's shirt, getting closer and closer to the edge of oblivion again.

"Mark me." Liam tilted his head to the side, giving permission, and nothing on the face of the earth would've stopped Declan from leaning forward and sinking his canines deep into Liam's throat, marking the man forever as his.

Declan screamed into Liam's neck, and he rocketed into another orgasm. Liam followed immediately behind him, his cock pulsing deep before the mating knot extended and attached itself to Declan. He moaned and shuddered once again in pleasure.

Declan removed his teeth from Liam's neck and licked the wound, starting the healing process, before he collapsed in Liam's arms, the world going black around him.

Chapter Ten

A week after Declan met Alpha Taylor, Ben managed to find an Alpha without a pack who'd be willing to make a move. Unfortunately, he had some business to settle and wouldn't be able to get away immediately. Declan spoke to his brother at least once a day, and so far he hadn't had any trouble with Alpha Wallis.

It took a lot of talking by his mate and Ben to convince Declan it would be safer for everyone if Tommy stayed in Cairns until everything got sorted. Wallis could be watching Tommy, and if he packed up and moved to Atherton, it would lead Alpha Wallis directly to Declan.

Declan couldn't return to Cairns until Wallis had been dealt with. That couldn't happen until Ben had verified all the facts. Obviously, the man couldn't appear to just take Declan's word about the murder. Ben dispatched Corey and Bradley down to Cairns for a number of days to discreetly poke around in the pack. It would be a calculated risk, both were known Betas, but Declan assumed Ben wouldn't need much time to make a move once he verified Alpha Wallis's true nature.

The Betas didn't come back with good news. Declan had no idea what they discovered and didn't press for an answer. It wasn't his place to ask questions. Liam, however, came home looking more and more stressed, and Declan didn't think it had anything to do with the construction company.

Declan didn't bug Liam about it. He only told his mate that if he wanted to talk, he would be there, but because of Liam's position as a Beta for his pack, Declan understood there would be times when Liam couldn't talk about might be going on.

Even with Liam's sombre moods and Declan's worry about his brother, the week had been the happiest Declan could remember. He fell more and more in love with his mate as the days passed. He didn't know if he could tell Liam how he felt considering they had only known each other for just over a week, but Declan decided waking up naked and wrapped up in his mate's arms would be a great way to start each day of his life. He hoped they got the opportunity.

Liam had taken Declan to meet his parents. As nervous as he'd been at meeting his mate's family, he enjoyed the night immensely. Judy and Henry Anderson were wonderful people, and if Declan's parents had survived, they would have liked them. Declan also met Liam's younger siblings, Christopher and Lila.

One of the few times Declan had seen Liam laugh during the week had been when Sam told Liam he couldn't play poker with them unless Declan brought some dessert or other confection. The game had taken place at Sam's, and Declan made a choc-hazelnut swirl cheesecake along with lemon and raspberry tartlets.

The desserts were deemed worthy, and the guys

questioned him about what would be on next week's menu.

Of course he refused to tell them.

Declan spent most of his days in the kitchen, while Liam worked on some building site. Declan had long ago realised he felt happiest when he could create some sweet or another. Liam always complimented the aromas wafting through the house when he arrived home. He never got angry when Declan ran out of ingredients and asked him to stop off at the store after he finished work. Declan also managed to win the hearts of Liam's workers by sending the various cakes, slices, biscuits, muffins, whatever took his fancy when he started cooking, with Liam when he left for work each day.

Right in the middle of sifting the self-raising flour for the chocolate slice he had decided to bake, the house phone rang. Declan hadn't seen the point in getting another mobile as he had a perfectly good one back in Cairns. He just couldn't get to it at the moment.

He stopped and picked up the phone, glancing at the display. Tommy's mobile. He clicked the green talk button and rested the phone between his shoulder and his ear so he could continue working

"Hey, Tommy, I'm in the middle of making your favourite slice." He started sifting flour again.

"Really, and what would that be?" The deep voice of his Alpha came through the line.

Declan dropped the sifter and watched in a daze

when flour exploded everywhere. The image of the last time Declan had seen Alpha Wallis flashed through his head, the sickening sound of the gun going off set on replay accompanying the images like a twisted soundtrack.

"Where's Tommy?" he asked quietly, nearly on the verge of tears.

"He's right here with me."

"Like I'm going to believe you," Declan said with more gusto than he felt.

The snarl on the other end of the line probably would have had Declan cowering if he had been in the same room with the man. "Fine, here."

A loud cry of pain echoed down the line as the phone exchanged hands. "Dec, I'm so sorry."

"Tommy," Declan yelled, but Alpha Wallis's laughter greeted his words.

"Now do you believe me?" he asked smugly.

"Yes," Declan croaked and tears started falling.

None of this would've happened if he hadn't left Tommy alone. He should have gone back and gotten his brother sooner instead of leaving him there unprotected.

"You just couldn't keep your fucking mouth shut, could you?" Alpha Wallis growled.

"I didn't tell anyone, I swear." Declan hoped it sounded like the truth.

"Don't fucking lie to me. Do you think I don't know about the wolves that have been poking their noses into my business? Huh?" The man sounded pissed, and it would only be a matter of time before Alpha Wallis lost his patience. "I'll make you a deal."

Whatever the man said, Declan more than likely wouldn't like it.

Alpha Wallis continued. "You get your ass back here and face the music, or your brother will. You have until six o'clock." The phone went dead in his ear.

Declan collapsed to the ground, uncaring of the flour everywhere, and sobbed. Alpha Wallis had Tommy. He couldn't let his little brother get hurt because of him.

"Honey, what's wrong, I can feel your pain. What's happened?" The soothing tones of his mate's voice floated through his mind.

Declan sobbed again before he could gather himself together enough to answer his mate. *"Alpha Wallis has Tommy."* He hiccupped and tried to calm himself down.

Falling into hysterics would not help Tommy.

"I'm leaving now. I'll call Ben on my way. I'll be home soon."

"Hurry, I've got till six tonight to get there before he kills Tommy."

"Hold it together, honey, Tommy needs you. I'll see you in five minutes."

Declan pulled his knees to his chest and wrapped his arms around them, trying to calm down. He couldn't lose Tommy. It had nearly killed them when their parents had been shot by poachers when they were out running together. He didn't think he would survive if Tommy was taken from him as well. He knew Liam would do everything within his power to help him.

Declan had no idea how long he'd been sitting huddled on the floor when a hand landed on his shoulder. Declan cried out, looking around wildly until his gaze settled on his mate.

"Shh, honey. Everything's okay. We're going to go get Tommy. Come on."

Liam helped Declan from the floor and pulled him tight to his chest. The scent of his mate surrounded him and did more to calm him than everything else he had tried since the phone call. Liam's strong arms gave him a feeling of utter safety, and Declan never wanted to give them up.

"I love you," he blurted.

Declan had had no idea the words were going to come out until it was too late. Embarrassed at his case of verbal diarrhoea, Declan buried his face in his mate's shirt.

Liam didn't laugh. Instead, he eased Declan back and lifted his head until he could look him in the eyes. "I love you too, Declan. Nothing and no one is going to take you away from me. Okay?"

Declan nodded and Liam laid a gentle kiss against his lips.

"Let's go get your brother and bring him home, hmm?"

"Yes, please," he whispered.

"Then we can all come back here and watch you clean up the kitchen. Damn, babe. It looks like a bag of flour exploded in here," Liam said.

Declan laughed as he looked around the room. Liam had it right. Flour covered just about every surface within a fairly large radius of where they stood.

"Thank you," he said.

Liam had taken his mind off Tommy for a moment, and he appreciated it.

"You're welcome. Now let's go. Hopefully Ben should be out the front waiting for us by now." Liam took Declan's hand, and they walked through the house and out the front door, which Liam had left open in his obvious haste to get to Declan.

Liam locked the door behind them and they headed to the big SUV Ben sat waiting in.

"Where to?" Ben asked when Liam climbed in to the front seat and Declan got in the back.

"Umm… he didn't say. Just that I had until six to take my brother's place." Declan looked at his watch. It had just gone four so they had time. "Knowing how much of an ass the man is, he probably thinks it's fitting to go back to the place where I witnessed Nigel's murder. So I guess that means the pack grounds in Cairns. Do you know where that is?"

"Yeah, Brad reported its whereabouts after his and Corey's scouting mission." Ben put the car in reverse and left the driveway.

As they drove, something Alpha Wallis said registered with Declan.

"He knows." He didn't realize he'd spoken aloud until Liam asked him.

"Who knows what?"

"Alpha Wallis, he knows about Corey and Brad. He told me on the phone about the wolves poking around his pack."

"Doesn't matter now. Everything's going to come to a head this afternoon. Alpha Wallis's time is up. Frank, Glen, and Adrian should be arriving in the next day or so anyway, so this wouldn't have gone on for much longer." Ben's anger was clearly evident in his voice.

Declan processed what Ben said and settled back against the seat as they headed towards Cairns.

He hadn't slept, but Declan must have zoned out, because the next thing he registered, the car pulled to a stop in his pack grounds' car park.

Declan exited the vehicle. As soon as his feet touched the ground, he started shivering. He had no idea why, the temperature felt pleasant, by no means cold yet.

Liam wrapped his arms around Declan, pulling him close. "Everything's going to be fine. Tommy will be fine. We'll go get him, kick the Alpha's ass, and go home. Okay?"

"Yeah." That sounded really good, in fact.

Ben came round the front of the car and waved his hand towards the trees. "Can you lead us to where everything went down?"

"Yeah." Declan didn't look forward to going back there.

Hell, he didn't want to walk back into the stretch of trees, full stop. Liam never let go of his hand as they headed into the bush.

Declan glanced down at his watch. Half past five. Shit, it had taken them longer to get here than he thought. They needed to move. After traipsing through the trees for maybe fifteen minutes, the sound of a gun reverberated through the silence. Birds screeched and took flight above them.

"Tommy!" Declan shouted, yanking his hand away from his mate's and racing through the trees.

He didn't care if Liam and Ben were behind him or not, once again thankful for his speed. His heart pounded in his chest and he pushed branches out of his way, ignoring the stinging cuts to his skin when he had been unsuccessful in moving them in time.

Declan finally broke through the edge into the same clearing where he had witnessed Nigel's murder. Time seemed to slow down as he came to a halt. Gregory and Barry held Tommy between them just as they had Nigel that night. Tommy sagged, naked, his body covered in bruises, his left leg broken, the bone sticking out through the skin. Declan couldn't see Tommy's face with his head slumped forward. Hell, he couldn't even tell from where he stood if his brother was alive or not.

He turned to face the Alpha, fury rolling through him. Before he could so much as utter a sound, the gun in Alpha Wallis's hand went off again and fiery pain pierced Declan's left shoulder. The force of the impact knocked him backwards to the ground. His head landed hard against a rock, and black spots danced before his eyes.

Twin howls rent the air when Liam and Ben burst through the tree line in their shifted form. If Tommy still breathed, Liam would rescue him. That was his last thought before he let the darkness take him.

* * * * *

Damn, but his mate could really run. Liam's heart nearly stopped when another gunshot rent the air. Fire rolled through his body. Not his own pain. Declan had been shot.

Shifting, Liam howled and broke through the tree line, Ben right beside him. Alpha Wallis stood in the centre of a clearing, the gun now pointing in their direction. Liam lowered his head and put on a burst of speed. He might not be nearly as fast as his mate, but he could still run with the best of them. Ben easily remained right beside him.

Alpha Wallis seemed to be having trouble deciding

who to shoot at first, finally deciding on Liam. He pulled the trigger again. At the last second, Liam veered to the left and headed to the Betas who were holding up Tommy between them.

As much as Liam wanted to take on Alpha Wallis, it would be better all-round if Ben did the honours. Liam liked being a Beta. He didn't want to be Alpha, and if he beat Kegan Wallis, and he would with the way he felt right now, he'd become Alpha of the Cairns pack. He didn't want that. He'd discussed the possibility at length with Ben over the last week. As much as he wanted to be the one to take out the man who had caused his mate so much grief, he couldn't.

He'd promised Declan he'd get his brother, and he planned to do exactly that. When the two Betas saw him heading directly for them, they took one look at their Alpha currently engaged in a fight with Ben and dropped Tommy to the ground and made a run for it.

Cowards. Liam watched them disappear into the tree line. He had more important things to do than give chase. They'd be caught eventually and held accountable for their crimes. At the moment he had other things to worry about. The sounds of fighting carried on behind him. Liam had no doubt Ben would come out of the encounter the victor.

He shifted and knelt down beside Tommy. Even through all the bruising, he could see the resemblance. Liam breathed a sigh of relief when he noticed Tommy's pulse beating under his skin. He didn't know where to touch the young man; his body was a mass of bruised and broken flesh, and Liam was afraid no matter where he placed his hands, it would cause Tommy more pain. Probably a good thing Tommy had passed out.

Liam tried to be as gentle as possible, but his breath caught in his throat when the mate threads between Declan's younger brother and Ben joined in his mind. Fuck! Not good. Declan would have a fit when he found out. Declan had nothing against Ben, but Tommy being Declan's much-younger brother would have all of his protective instincts coming out. Liam and Declan had talked at length about his little brother and how Declan had raised him after their parents passed. He didn't know if Declan could let go of that mindset, especially after what had just happened.

Looking down once again at the bruised and battered body of his mate's brother, he had no idea how his friend and Alpha would react either. It would have to wait, though. At the moment, he needed to get back to his mate and make sure he was okay.

Liam picked Tommy up in his arms, trying not to hurt the young man any more than he already had been, and started back across the field towards where his mate lay.

"Honey, come on, wake up, please," Liam asked soothingly as they got closer. He didn't receive any response.

The fighting had diminished, and when Liam laid Tommy beside Declan, Ben made his way over to them.

Liam checked out his mate. The bullet had made one hell of a mess of his shoulder, but it looked like a through and through, thank God. They wouldn't have to go digging around to remove the bullet. As bad as the wound looked, it would have been worse when it first happened. Liam wished the healing could go faster, but he'd be happy with whatever he got.

Ben arrived and crouched on the other side of Liam. His muzzle and back left leg were both covered in blood, and he had a large gouge in his flank.

"Shift, Alpha," Liam said quietly to his friend.

As soon as Ben realized his mate had been found but remained gravely injured, he'd lose his shit. And Liam needed him to keep it together. Ben's head snapped up, and he sniffed the air several times before he made his way to Tommy's side. Ben lay down and licked Tommy's face before raising his muzzle and howling the most haunted sound Liam had ever heard.

Liam watched in wonder when Tommy's faint mate thread seemed to strengthen simply with the Alpha being so close to him. Every time Ben nuzzled Tommy, the partially joined threads pulsed with energy and Liam held out hope for the future. The threads wouldn't join completely until after the pair had claimed one another, but that could happen later. Now, they needed to get Tommy and Declan somewhere they could heal in peace.

"He's alive, Ben. Now shift and we can get them out of here," Liam said sharply.

Liam held back his surprise when Ben obeyed him immediately. The tall, macho Alpha seemed to crumble when he took in the extent of his young mate's injuries. Ben picked Tommy up in his arms with more care than Liam had ever seen the Alpha use.

Liam did the same with Declan and the pair was soon on their way back through the trees. Ben didn't say anything the entire walk, too busy paying attention to the man he held in his arms, not that Liam blamed him.

When they exited the tree line, Liam opened the passenger door and settled Declan in, strapping him in place with the seatbelt. Liam then opened the back door so Ben could lay Tommy down before he headed to the rear of the SUV. Opening up the back, he pulled out the bag Ben always kept with spare garments of all sizes. Shifters never knew when they would be in need of more clothes.

He threw Ben a pair of jeans and a shirt. Unfortunately there were no spare shoes in the car. Theirs were back in the forest somewhere, and Liam didn't plan to go looking for them. Liam pulled on a pair of sweats and a shirt before he threw the bag in the back and closed the door. Ben climbed awkwardly into the back seat so he could be with his mate. The man stood six foot six and was not really built for back seats.

Liam got in the driver's side and, after checking on

his mate, headed the car in the direction of home.

The drive home went as quietly as the walk back to the car. About fifteen minutes from Atherton, Liam decided he better broach a subject he really didn't want to.

He cleared his throat. "Ben?"

Ben grunted.

Figuring that would be the best he'd get, he continued, "You realise Tommy won't be going home with you? Right?"

"Excuse me?"

The low rumbling growl from his Alpha had Liam's hairs standing up all over his body. Liam had to grit his teeth not to bend his head and expose his neck.

"Ben, he's young. Ten years younger than Declan. And he's just been abused. The last thing he needs is to wake up in a strange house with a strange man. He needs his brother. Please understand." Liam hoped he could get his Alpha to see reason. He hated having to be the one to keep his Alpha from taking his mate home, but he honestly thought it for the best.

Ben snorted and went back to caressing Tommy's face. Liam knew Declan would have a fit if Tommy went home with Ben at the moment. He had no idea how his lover would deal with the situation, but he thought it best for all involved if Tommy came home with them to begin with.

Liam handed Ben his phone from the centre console.

"You might want to call Dr Carter and have him meet us at my place."

"Shit," Ben muttered before placing the call. "He'll meet us there in ten," Ben said as he ended the conversation.

Liam nodded and quickly looked at his mate again. If not for the blood-soaked shirt, one could think he slept peacefully. Waking up this morning, Liam had no idea of the shit fest this day would turn out to be. He was glad his friend and Alpha had finally met his mate, even if they did have a long road ahead of them.

Epilogue

Two Months Later

"Mmmm." Declan moaned and pressed back against the hard shaft currently trying to pierce his body. His eyes fluttered open and he twisted his head to the side.

"Morning, love." He met Liam's mouth in a lazy kiss.

"Morning yourself," Liam whispered and his shaft broke through Declan's guardian muscle.

Liam took it slow, no need to rush. Saturday morning dawned and neither of them needed to be anywhere.

Declan pushed back when Liam withdrew his huge cock and slowly rocked forward once again. Liam reached around and gripped Declan's aching length.

He started a maddening pace that matched his thrusts. Declan relaxed against Liam's chest and let his mate have his way with him. His body sung as desire built, and his balls drew tight against his body.

Declan panted and gripped Liam's hip behind him as his mate continued to rock into him. Liam squeezed his fist tight and bit deep into the side of his neck, and Declan flew over the edge, tumbling freely, as he gave his body over to the ministrations of his mate. Pearly white cum shot from his cock, covering his stomach and Liam's hand. His mate thrust hard two more time before going still, his low groan muffled by Declan's neck as his cock twitched deep within the confines of Declan's body.

They lay together, relaxing in each other's arms until their bodies released them from their knotted embrace. Declan whimpered when Liam's softened cock slipped from his body, but he rolled over and kissed his mate properly.

"Good morning."

"Morning, love. Shower?" Liam asked.

Hmm. His mate, naked and wet? He couldn't think of anything better.

Declan lay in bed for a little while so Liam could get the shower started. His thoughts, as they inevitably did, went to his brother. Tommy had finally woken up the day after they had brought him back to Atherton and cried while Declan held him close. In broken sobs Tommy recounted what he remembered of his ordeal. Declan's heart ached for his brother. He hated his former Alpha for destroying Tommy's youthful exuberance.

His brother had changed. He spent the majority of his days alone, quiet and withdrawn. He jumped at shadows and constantly woke throughout the night, screaming from nightmares. Declan would do anything he could to help Tommy deal with what had happened.

Tommy wasn't ready to mate Ben yet. Once Tommy stopped being so afraid, Declan hoped things would change. He still lived with Declan and Liam. Ben understood and willingly gave Tommy all the time he needed. Thank God. It didn't stop the man from coming round constantly or calling to check up on Tommy, though.

Declan couldn't blame the Alpha and thought it actually kind of sweet. He just hoped Tommy would come round and see Ben for the loving, caring man Declan had come to know.

Frank Schmidt had taken over the Cairns pack with his two Betas, Glen and Adrian. They had found and dealt with Gregory and Barry. Declan had no idea how they handled it, but he trusted Liam when he said there would be no more trouble from them.

The police had received an anonymous tip about the former Alpha's house. When they searched it, drugs and money totalling nearly half a million were found. Declan had no idea where Wallis had gotten it all, but at least it wouldn't make it to the streets.

Kegan Wallis's mauled body had been discovered in the woods on the opposite side of town a week after Ben had killed him, officially closing the police investigation. His death had been ruled an animal attack. The detectives had no idea how right they were.

Liam had dropped a bomb on him the previous week when he had told Declan they couldn't have sex for the day. When he asked why, Liam explained that, once mated, there was the possibility of getting pregnant if they made love on the day of the new moon. Declan still had trouble wrapping his brain around that little piece of information but thought it wouldn't completely be out of the realm of possibility for them and their future. He would love nothing more than to give his mate the family he had always wanted, but never voiced.

"Babe, are you coming?" Liam called out from the bathroom.

"No, but I will be shortly," Declan mumbled under his breath as he got out of bed and headed towards his mate, happy in the knowledge that no matter what life threw at him, Liam would be by his side.

Always.

The End

Dear Reader

Thank you for downloading *Liam*. We hope you enjoyed this new pack extension of the Holland Brother Universe. Toni loves being able to have more wolves around. (And who can blame her? Sexy boys.)

Want more Atherton Pack? Toni currently has three books out in the series and another in the planning stages. And if your a paranormal lover, you may also want to give Mathilde Watson's *BULL* a spin—because it will give you one if you can stay on!

Want to hear the latest news about Toni and other Mischiefer releases and titles? Join our newsletter (and receive a FREE book!)

Want to let us know what you think? Please consider leaving a review where you purchased this ebook or on Goodreads. Reviews and word-of-mouth recommendations are *vital* to independent publishers.

Sincerely,
Mischief Corner Books

About Toni Griffin

Toni Griffin lives in Darwin, the smallest of Australia's capital cities. Born and raised in the state she's a Territorian through and through. Growing up Toni hated English with a passion (as her editors can probably attest to) and found her strength lies with numbers.

Now, though, she loves escaping to the worlds she creates and hopes to continue to do so for many years to come. She's a single mother of one and works full time. When she's not writing you can just about guarantee that she will be reading one of the many MM authors she loves.

Feel free to drop her a line at info@tonigriffin.net anytime.

Facebook:
http://www.facebook.com/toni.griffin.author

Webpage:
http://www.tonigriffin.net

Also by Toni Griffin

Available from **Mischief Corner Books**

My Christmas Present
Once a Cowboy

SMOKEY MOUNTAIN BEARS
A Bear in the Woods
Wreath of Fire

HOUNDS OF HELL
Archie's Accidental Kidnapping

THE BORILLIAN TWIST
Finding Connor

THE HOLLAND BROTHERS
Unexpected Mate
Determined Mate
Protective Mate
Forbidden Mate
A Very Holland Christmas
A Very Holland Valentine

THE ATHERTON PACK
Liam
Ben
Corey

Available from **Extasy Books**

TASSIE WOLVES
Hidden Wolf

THE THOMPSON AGENCY
Dealing with the Dead
Dealing with the Past

Available from **Amber Allure**

HOT ENCOUNTERS
Frankie's Vamp
Bryce's Cop

About Mischief Corner Books

Mischief Corner Books is an organization of superheroes... no, it's a platinum-album techno-fusion group... no, hold on a sec here...

Ah yes. Mischief Corner Books is a diverse group of authors who met on a mountain in Tennessee and decided since they were probably too easily distracted to rule the world that they'd settle for causing a bit of mayhem instead.

In addition to making mayhem, we publish books with a diverse range of genres and topics... we live to break molds.

MCB. Giving voice to LGBTQ fiction.

Website:
http://www.mischiefcornerbooks.com

Printed in Great Britain
by Amazon